OFF THE HOOK: SECOND EDITION

A PETER PAN RETELL, CLEAN ROMANCE NOVEL

MINDY LEMIEUX

ISBN print: 979-8-9997942-0-8

ISBN ebook: 979-8-9997942-1-5

Editing by KaTrina Jackson of Eschler Editing, and Andrew J. LeMieux, Esq.

Cover design by Eschler Editing (didn't they do an awesome job?)

Printed and bound in the United States of America

First printing October 15, 2025

Published by Mindy LeMieux

Dedicated to everyone who's ever needed a second chance.

CONTENTS

PROLOGUE

Wendy stared at the granite marker. *George and Mary Darling—beloved parents of Wendy, John, and Michael.*

Sorrow curdled in her stomach. They had the best doctors available, but it was in vain. The fever had taken their parents far too soon. She put an arm around John and Michael, who both stood a head taller than her now.

The rain-soaked tree they stood under periodically shed drops of water on their heads, and tears rolled down her brothers' faces, just as rain rolled down the grave markers. She hugged her brothers tight. At least they had each other.

Michael stiffened. Wendy turned to him to see him staring pointedly in the distance. She followed his gaze to see a figure of average height dressed in a dark overcoat approaching and, unbidden, her heart quickened. She hadn't thought it was possible, but he'd grown.

"Peter," she whispered. She strode toward him, her brothers following. A moment later, the four of them embraced, holding each other wordlessly for a time.

Wendy let out a sob.

"Hush there now," Peter coaxed in his light British accent. "You're not alone." He pulled back and faced them, his green eyes filled with concern. "I'm sorry about your parents." He looked each of them in the eyes before continuing. "I mourn for you, and I wish to mourn *with* you."

Wendy exchanged befuddled expressions with her brothers. He wished to mourn *with* them? What did he mean by that?

Peter's mouth was set in a firm line. "This may be too soon to suggest, but listen. Come away with me to Neverland. Let me and the Lost Boys be your family. Let Neverland be your home. Leave London and time behind." His eyes brightened as he smiled. "Come with me. There are more adventures to be had."

Wendy felt her brother's eyes on her. Peter's idea was tempting. Maybe they should leave England and their heartache behind. The idea of additional adventures with Peter and the Lost Boys lifted the perpetual cloud that had hovered over her since her parents' deaths.

She glanced up at her teenage brothers. Their expressions said they were already set on this proposal. There wasn't much left for them here with their parents gone.

Wendy turned to Peter. "When do we leave?"

～

Much time seemed to have passed since the Darling siblings had returned to Neverland.

Time, thought Hook derisively. *This is Neverland. There's no accounting of time here.*

He crouched behind a moss-covered boulder and strained to hear Wendy's words as she argued with Peter, again, about returning to what she called Reality. He'd made a habit of slipping away from his ship to observe Peter and his group, and the arguments he held with Wendy had become entertaining.

He saw Peter throw his head back and whine. "Why not just stay here?"

Wendy's eyebrow lifted, a sure sign of her solid comeback. Hook had seen her use it on Peter multiple times. "Neverland is the same thing every day," she pointed out. "It's wearisome watching you play hero all the time. We can't do this for the rest of our lives."

Peter's head pulled back. "We? You mean, *all* of you?"

Wendy, her brothers, and the Lost Boys nodded together.

Hook raised an eyebrow. *What a curious development.*

"We've even got the ship ready to go," John supplied, which earned him a scowl from Peter.

Wendy sighed. "We've gone over this before, Peter. And we want you to come with us. It would be a new adventure."

Hook smiled. Wendy had used the magic word on Peter: *Adventure*.

Peter crossed his arms and regarded the group with a clenched jaw. "Fine," he said after a period of silence.

The group cheered, triggering an idea in Hook's mind. Wendy's intriguing debates with Peter, which Hook had watched from a hidden distance, certainly held merit. Now he, too, wanted to leave this place. He formed a plan to make that happen.

Neverland truly was the same experience day after day—fight with Peter, avoid the crocodile, manage his pirate crew, and remain stuck in this place and lifestyle forever. But no more.

Why be a villain? Hook dreamed of a peaceful life devoid of piracy and fighting Peter and the Lost Boys. Perhaps there could be a wife and family in his future. But that would never happen here.

Hook regarded Wendy, who had developed incredibly during the years she and her brothers had grown up in London. She appeared to be nearly twenty now, not too far from his early-twenty-something in age, at least by appearance.

He took in her delicate features, her blue eyes filled with intelligence, her long honey-colored hair, and her regal stature. He admired who she had become and hoped he could find someone like her wherever they landed and started over. Someone *like* her, because there would never be a chance between him and Wendy. How could she love a villain?

Hook shook his head to free his thoughts and watched as Peter stomped away from Wendy and the others, shouting over his shoulder as he went, "I'm going to see Tink!"

Hook saw Wendy blink in relief before turning to her brothers and the Lost Boys. "Go pack your things. We shall depart in the morning."

Hook's heart sped up. Morning didn't leave him much time to prepare to flee Neverland.

He inched away from his hiding place and made his way to his new ship, since Peter had stolen the *Jolly Roger* and doused it with pixie dust.

Hook stayed in his lavish quarters for the rest of the day and into the night, with firm orders that his crew leave him to his solitude.

What should he bring with him to Reality? He pulled out anything of value and stuffed the items in a leather satchel.

What should he leave behind? His crew, most definitely. How could he start a new life with a horde of unruly men who fought with children? No, he'd leave on his own.

As he fastened the satchel closed, his eyes landed on his hook.

He used his left hand to push down and gave a firm twist on his hook, releasing it from the mechanism on his arm. He took in the curve of the metal and the deadly point at the end, which he'd sharpened every night.

He shifted it in his left hand, pulled his arm back, and hurled the hook across his quarters. The pointed end embedded itself into the wooden wall with a satisfying *thunk*.

"Thus perished Captain Hook," he whispered before turning toward his window. "And thus revived Evander Roberts."

He slipped out his gilded window, eased himself down a rope, and landed in a rowboat he'd positioned below his window earlier. With quiet strokes, he made his way to shore. Then he stole through the forest to Peter's flying ship and deftly crept into the cargo hold.

Hook smirked and chuckled to himself, shaking his head and brushing his dark hair across his eyebrows. He never thought he'd be a stowaway, but here he was. He didn't know what any of them would find once they landed, but it had to be better than their current situation.

He was literally sitting in the dark, and proverbially taking a leap into the dark, by leaving Neverland.

He settled himself in a corner behind several barrels, and at some point, fell asleep.

He awoke to the sound of Peter's voice from the deck. "Ready to fly, boys?"

"Ready, Peter!" they shouted back.

The ship began to move, and a few crates and boxes teetered from above, nearly landing on Hook. He lifted his arms overhead and took hold of a beam to steady himself. Then he closed his eyes and took a deep breath.

He was ready to move forward with his life.

CHAPTER ONE

Peter sat at work thinking about the day he left Neverland three years ago. He wondered (for the umpteenth time) how in the world the ship had landed the group of him, Wendy and her brothers, and the Lost Boys in this place and at this time of Earth's history. Last he'd checked, the ship only knew the way to England, roughly ending up around the end of the nineteenth century. Yet here he was in the United States of America in the twenty-first century.

Who would have guessed? he thought to himself. The USA wasn't so bad, he supposed. At least they'd landed in a place with woods, mountains, and bodies of water—there was plenty to explore to satisfy his thirst for adventure. And this century certainly had its perks. One couldn't deny that indoor plumbing was a welcome advancement.

But the need to *work* to support oneself. He could certainly do without that. Scheduling clients for outdoor treks in a cramped cabin really wasn't his style, being the designated leader he'd always been. He should be the one taking people on the outdoor treks. But that required more education and training. He shuddered at the thought of studying.

Oh well. At least he had something to look forward to once he finished work that day. Wendy would be buying him a pastry.

Pastries were a happy thought indeed, though even the happiest of happy thoughts couldn't help him fly in Reality. He still tried on occasion. He presently sat at his uneventful desk and filled his mind with happy thoughts, but he didn't make it off his old, upholstered seat one bit.

He was pulled out of his meandering thoughts when the desk phone rang. He shook his head and answered it. "Outdoor Adventure Trek," he droned. "This is Peter."

Hadn't his boss ever heard of online scheduling?

He sighed after the call ended, then tilted his neck from side to side before finishing the client notes in the office appointment book. The anticipated confection from Wendy acted like a carrot hanging from a stick to keep him motivated. How could anyone work without promised rewards?

⁓

Wendy sat at a table staring at her empty water cup and waited for Peter for their monthly rendezvous. At least, *she* liked to think of it as a rendezvous since that sounded romantic. And meeting at a French bakery—well, the French were known for romance. Her childhood crush on Peter still held, though she was now a grown woman in her early twenties.

As a young girl, she'd found Peter adorably handsome when he'd first flown into her room in London and taken her to Neverland. And now he'd grown into an undeniably attractive man. The hero-worship she'd long felt for him, combined with his captivating features and strong form, pulled Wendy in as metal draws in a magnet.

If only he felt the same draw for her.

She knew that for Peter, their "hanging out," as he called it, was merely a good excuse to land a free treat.

One way to a man's heart is through his stomach, Wendy thought. If only that held true for Peter.

So, each month Peter would join her at the bakery for a pastry. Though seldom on time.

Wendy glanced at her watch and realized she'd been waiting for him for nearly thirty minutes. Her lunch hour from the pediatric clinic would be over soon.

Aren't I worth being on time for? she wondered as she played with the end of her ponytail and tapped her fingers on her blue scrubs.

She noticed movement at the entrance and saw Peter swaggering his way toward her. He wore a dark gray T-shirt that hugged his chest and showed his well-defined muscles, denim jeans, and a leather jacket. His smile cocked up to one side when he spotted her. She sat up straighter, her smile brightening at the sight of his wickedly handsome appearance.

"Catch," he said as he approached her. He pulled something from his back pocket and tossed it at Wendy.

She shrieked and flew back from her chair. Everyone in the bakery turned to look while Peter stood next to their table laughing. A man approached and lifted the long, scaly abomination from the table. "It's fake, miss," he explained while waving a rubber snake in his hands. Peter snatched the snake back with a smirk and took a seat next to a very embarrassed Wendy.

"Why would you do that?" she hissed at him. Would his childishness ever stop?

"Oh, come now, Wendy. It was only a joke." Peter waved his hand. "Show me what sort of pastry you found for me today." He slid his chair next to her at their table.

She scowled at him, and after her pulse slowed, she pulled out a white pastry box. "Perhaps I'll keep it for myself today, after what you did."

Peter shrugged. "It wasn't that bad."

"I'm *terrified* of snakes, Peter."

He straightened with wide eyes. "You are?"

She glared at him. He already knew that. There had been too many incidents with snakes in Neverland for him to forget.

"What if you just show me what's in the box instead?" Peter's eyes focused on the pastry box.

Wendy huffed but told herself to relax—she'd already caused a scene. "It's a French Walnut Tart. Did you know it takes nearly three hours to make? That's what the pastry chef told me while I waited for you."

Peter inspected the tart and his expression deflated.

"It has nuts in it?" he whined. "Who puts nuts into a perfectly good pastry?"

He made a disgusted face and shook his head, his auburn hair sweeping his forehead with the motion. He stared at Wendy with his captivating green eyes, all seriousness.

"Wendy, you know I don't like nuts."

And you know I don't like snakes, she thought in rebuttal as she fought the urge to roll her eyes.

But, as Peter often put up a protest to new things, his childish reaction didn't surprise her, though it was exasperating.

"Yes," she countered in a smooth voice. "But the tart also contains caramel, and I know you *love* that." She winked at him, though she tried to quell the frustration rising in her.

His attractiveness aside, whenever they were together, some kind of argument always surfaced. The thought pinched her chest. She had hoped that by this point—now that they were both in their early-twenties (at least, that's what Peter looked like)—they'd be past childish disagreements.

"Oh, fine," he conceded with a huff. He flopped his elbows onto the table and held his hand out for Wendy to hand him a fork. "But *please* remember the things I like next time. I look forward to this every month, you know."

"Our meeting together?" A fluttering came to life in her midsection and her annoyance dissolved. Perhaps a romance between them was in sight after all.

"The food," Peter answered over a mouthful. Apparently having nuts wasn't as awful as he'd fussed about. Things usually weren't as awful as Peter fussed about.

Wendy felt her facial expression fall, and her hope of romance dropped a few notches. Peter sat chewing for a moment before realization struck his features.

"The food *and* our meeting together. Of course I look forward to seeing you, Wendy." He leaned back, crossed his arms, and disarmed her with his smile.

11

Wendy relaxed as her hopes rose again. She truly appreciated having his full attention, which happened rarely. But even his full attention was tenuous.

His head swiveled to the left, his eyes pulling away from Wendy toward a woman around their age at the bakery counter. He flashed her a dashing smile and then winked. The young woman hid a flirtatious grin behind her hand as she strode past them and out the door.

After watching her retreating form, he turned back to Wendy with an amused expression.

But Wendy was not amused.

Her hopes plummeted. Would he ever grow up? First the snake, and now this. Would he ever think of anyone but himself?

"Seriously, Peter? Staring and flirting with her," she flung her hand toward the door, "when I'm right here?" She hit the table with her palm. Peter flinched, and a few heads turned in their direction again.

But she wasn't finished yet. "Am I just some convenient friend of yours? It's like we haven't known each other since my childhood, and we haven't been through the wildest experiences together. It's as though I'm just some other girl who ought to adore you, simply because you're attractive, smart, and confident." She swept her hand up and down to indicate the whole of him. "Is that how you see me?"

Wendy's breathing became quick and shallow as her frustration and hurt grew. She took a few deep breaths to calm herself. She'd hoped he'd own up to his rude behavior, even though she knew it was a foolish hope. He never did.

Peter regarded her for about three seconds. "So, you think I'm attractive, eh?" He waggled his eyebrows, grinning from ear-to-ear. He leaned back in his chair, crossed one ankle over his other knee, and waited for her answer.

She huffed before pushing her chair back and picking up her bag, intent on ending this ridiculous conversation. He shouldn't be mocking her.

"Wendy, calm down," Peter said with a laugh. He reached out and took hold of her arm.

Wendy reluctantly complied. "Don't you grow tired of childish games?"

"But they're games I always win," he answered, lifting one corner of his mouth.

Wendy scrunched her eyes in frustration and shook her head.

"I was only joking. You're right—you deserve better," Peter said placatingly.

Wendy opened her eyes to find Peter's face theatrically contrite.

She took another deep breath and closed her eyes. As she opened them, she intensified her glare, assessing his sincerity. She wanted to think the best of him, so she gave a quick nod in acceptance of his apology. Wait—did he even apologize?

"What's that in your bag?" Peter pointed to a folded paper sticking out of the top, effectively interrupting her thoughts.

She pulled the paper out and unfolded it, willing to shift their conversation. "I thought we might enjoy this class together."

The top of the flyer read "Fencing Lessons" in bold black lettering.

Peter scrunched his eyebrows. "Fencing lessons? This is ridiculous—I already know how to fence." He let out an indulgent chuckle. "And I'm rather good at it, if I do say so myself."

13

"Yes, but how long has it been since you wielded a sword?" She leaned forward and raised an eyebrow. She knew he detested that gesture—it meant she had a valid point in an argument.

He held out his hand for the paper, which Wendy handed over. His eyes scanned the flyer. "Who is Evan Roberts and why should we take lessons from him?" He looked up at Wendy and handed the flyer back to her. "Do you know him?"

Wendy shook her head. "No, my coworker at the clinic gave it to me earlier this week. It sparked memories of our adventures in," —here she dropped her voice to a whisper— "Neverland," she finished. "I thought it would be fun to do it together."

Peter sat up straight and adopted an air of superiority. "Something like this in modern-day society is useless. It's for little boys who wish to pretend to adventure." He waved his hand as though swatting at a fly.

"Peter, *you* were a little boy pretending to adventure—with sword fighting," Wendy countered, raising that challenging eyebrow again. "Are you scared you might be outdone by the instructor?"

"I'm not scared of anything. Unlike people who fear reptiles."

"It's just snakes. I'm fine with every other reptile." She involuntarily scanned their surroundings for the limbless ground dwellers before turning back to Peter. "You've changed the subject."

"I'm simply thinking it might be embarrassing for the instructor," Peter supplied.

"The instructor?" Wendy asked, her eyebrows coming together. "How would you being there be embarrassing for him?"

"I'm better at sword fighting. It would be embarrassing for him if one of his students was better than him." He pushed his chair away from the table, marking the end of their discussion.

Wendy smirked. She had him right where she wanted him. "*That* remains to be seen."

Peter stopped and turned to her, his dark auburn eyebrows almost touching. "Yes, it does." Then he leaned back. "But no promises. I might be off camping, or something."

Peter's attention was again pulled away as another woman caught his eye. He stood and waved. "Farewell." He then trotted out the door after her.

Wendy watched him leave and the spark in her heart dwindled to a pitiful ember. She glanced at the time on her phone and realized she'd be late returning to the clinic.

With a sigh, she picked up her bag and left the bakery. It shouldn't be this difficult to simply be friends with Peter, let alone establish a romantic relationship with him. Her hopes of what that looked like had waned over the years.

She would take what she could get. She smiled sadly. Maybe she had convinced Peter to take fencing lessons with her, maybe she hadn't. Only time would tell.

But why was it so difficult to get to that point? Why were things so arduous with him? And why did she feel so insignificant in his presence?

CHAPTER TWO

Wendy drove home after work thinking about her brothers. She admired how much they had grown since returning to Reality—both in stature and maturity.

John, around age twenty, had finished high school and now worked at the city library while taking night classes in biology. Michael, around age seventeen, was in his junior year in high school, working part time and saving for college. Though John and Michael were brothers, their appearance and mannerisms were a study in contrasts.

John towered over most people, his limbs long and lean. Dark hair made his pale skin stand out, with a smattering of freckles across his straight nose. He'd traded his glasses for contacts when he discovered they existed. ("This is the greatest invention ever," he exclaimed when wearing them for the first time.) His blue eyes were noticeably brighter without the glasses. And though he was a handsome man, he was too oblivious to notice. Truth be told, John was oblivious to many things.

Michael stood about shoulder-height to his brother, though he was still taller than Wendy. He was built broad and strong like his father, with honey-colored hair and discerning brown eyes like his mother. Though more soft-spoken than John, his face held an excitement about life. And despite being handsome in his own way, he was too humble to admit it.

The one certain similarity they shared was their love for their sister.

The thought warmed Wendy's heart as she entered their shared townhouse and found her brothers studying in the front room. She saw John straighten from his seat on the couch. His eyes brightened as the door closed behind her.

"Wendy!" he cheered, raising his hands in the air. "Come sit with us. We were just finishing our studies for the day." He closed his textbook while Michael put away his notebook.

Wendy hung her bag on the coat stand next to the door. "How was your day, boys?"

"Men," John called. "We're not boys anymore, Wendy."

Michael snickered while he and John shared a look.

"What is it?" Wendy asked, smiling curiously at them.

"John fancies a girl," Michael informed her.

"Michael," John censured his brother, who shrugged.

"Ooh, tell us about her," Wendy begged. It'd been months since he'd last been on a date.

John huffed dramatically. "I truly do fancy her, but I'd rather tell you more when I know if she reciprocates my feelings. Tell us about your day, Wendy."

Wendy sighed with satisfaction at her brother's love intrigue. Her thoughts turned to Peter and her longing to be exclusive with him.

John observed her from his seat on the couch. "You look as though you're sorting through a complex medical procedure."

Wendy sat next to him. "I simply wonder whatever possessed us to leave England?"

John's mouth pinched. "We left England to heal. Then we all chose to leave Neverland to progress. And now we're here." He paused, frowning. "I thought we'd all come to terms with how things happened."

Michael sat on the opposite couch. "But that doesn't mean we made a wrong choice in either situation. So much good has come of it. And we still have each other."

She nodded at Michael's words and shifted deeper into the couch while considering their answers.

"You're both happy here, then?" she asked.

"Indeed." John smiled.

She turned to her other brother. "Michael?"

"Truly," he responded while leaning forward. "Think about this location, this time in history. Machinery and science, Wendy. Man has been to the *moon*. The technology here is the stuff of novels we read as children. And indoor plumbing—"

"Amen to that," John inserted.

"The ease of transportation. And we have these." He pulled out his smart phone from his pocket. "Information at our fingertips. Literally."

Wendy's gaze fell to the floor in contemplation. "Yes, there are many reasons." Forcing a smile on her face, she leaned forward to stand from the couch.

"Wendy." Michael's voice held concern. "Are *you* happy here?"

"Of course," she reassured him with a soft smile. "For all the reasons you explained. I love being a nurse, where we live is wonderful, we've met some lovely people. And I have both of you."

"What more could you wish for?" John stood and placed a hand on her back.

There was one more thing her heart desired.

"I wish Peter would grow up." She looked back at her brothers, who shared deflated expressions, before heading to her room upstairs.

CHAPTER THREE

Wat becomes of a man who turns his life around completely, giving up the familiar for something challenging, though infinitely better? Evander Roberts, or Evan, as he was known in Reality, was fortunate enough to find out.

He shifted his stance under the weight of the large dresser he and his twenty-something year old coworker, Coby, were slowly carrying up a flight of stairs.

Though missing his right hand, physical labor satisfied Evan's soul and gave him the opportunity to think and reflect.

He'd created a proper life after leaving Neverland. The location and time they'd landed in were unexpected, but not undesirable. And he was thrilled to take advantage of the opportunity for a new life.

Evan's goals to reform had come along well. As Captain Hook, anger had been second nature to him, so he'd taken anger management classes to retrain his brain and keep his temper in check.

He'd attended Alcoholics Anonymous to drum away his thirst for alcohol. Being drunk took away his inhibitions and he wanted that gone from his life.

He'd found an honest line of work, a clean place to live, and made a few friends. Each day was a new horizon.

His mind wandered again to Wendy, wondering what she was doing with her life. If she was happy with Peter.

He wanted her to be happy. He'd admired her from a distance in Neverland.

I suppose I'm admiring her from a distance here too, he thought.

"Watch this last step," Coby warned in his deep American voice.

Being in the moving business was a profitable line of work with developing communities spreading far and wide in this part of the United States.

His side job as a fencing teacher brought in a modest income and it gave him pleasure to see his students progress from entry level to mastery. It served as a reminder of what he left behind, and what he worked for each day.

Evan and Coby made it to the top of the staircase, moved down the hallway, and into the room where the dresser would be placed. Carefully, they lowered it to the ground, then exhaled as they stood.

Evan stretched his arms overhead, then tilted his head side to side to loosen the strained muscles in his neck. Coby put his hands on his hips and twisted his torso from side to side, before surveying the room.

"Was that the last piece of furniture?" Coby wiped sweat from his forehead with a handkerchief.

"I believe so. The boxes are next."

"I need a break first." Coby stretched an arm.

They made their way down the stairs and out the front door.

Evan shaded his eyes from the sun with his left hand, the other having been severed from his body and fed to the infamous crocodile in Neverland. He then went to the front cab of the moving van, pulling out a bag with food and bottled water. When Coby came out of the house, they ate and drank in silence on the curb for a few minutes.

"You sure you won't join this next round of lessons?" Evan asked as he stared at the mature sycamore tree across the street. He'd invited Coby for several months to his fencing class, though each invitation had proven unsuccessful. He hadn't given up yet though.

"No thanks, my friend." Coby shook his head. "Brings back weird memories."

"Shame. You're young and strong. Seems as though you'd be right agile with a sword."

Coby cocked his head to peer at Evan, his brown curls hanging a bit over his eyes. His smile lit up his whole face. "I'm wicked with a sword, dude. Played at it all the time as a kid. I'm not too sharp in the noggin," he tapped the side of his head, "but I was good at that. I don't know about doing it again though."

Coby stared forward, deep in thought. "Is it hard to teach with just one hand?"

Evan shook his head. "I've been without it for so long that it would be strange to have it back. I'm used to doing things without it." He lifted the stump where his right arm ended at the wrist.

Coby bit his lower lip. "Tell me again how you lost it. You've told me before, but . . ."

"You forgot," Evan filled in at the same time Coby said, "I forgot."

"Childhood accident, you could say." Evan scowled at the memory, fresh anger toward Peter Pan rising. He hadn't entertained that memory since arriving in Reality. He shut his eyes, catching himself before

22

his anger grew. Using a breathing technique he'd learned in his anger management class, his temper subsided and he was in control of his emotions again.

He sat for a few breaths longer, then stood. "Let's finish with these boxes. Maybe we can head home early if we work fast enough."

"I bet I can carry in more than you this time," Coby challenged as he stood.

Evan smirked. "We shall see."

As Coby headed toward the back of the moving van he turned. "Childhood accident, huh? I got hurt a lot as a kid. We didn't have a lot of adult supervision." He shook his head and jumped up into the back of the truck to heft the boxes.

Evan made no response as he turned his attention to the remaining boxes. He could move more than Coby if he focused.

Chapter Four

It wasn't as though Peter *hated* where he worked, but he would love to boast that he started such a business. It could be a future goal, but goals required change. And why change his life when it functioned well enough?

Answering calls and scheduling clients gave him little pleasure, but a certain perk kept him coming in each day—access to an entire stock of everything one needed for outdoor excursions: gear for hiking, rock climbing, rowing, rafting, camping, fishing, and other outdoor activities. All this was available for clients to rent, but for employees, it was free.

This weekend was one of those instances where he took advantage of the free gear. Spring in the woods nearby was a sight to behold. Between the clear river and the scent of foliage waking up after the winter season, it was the perfect time to go on a camping excursion. Peter met up with John, Michael, and their friends formerly known as the Lost Boys.

They no longer went by their Neverland names of Tootles, Slightly, Nibs, and Curly.

Thomas (Tootles) was in law school with the hope of one day becoming a judge.

Slater (Slightly) had always been keen on music and was thick into it at college.

Nick (Nibs) had become adept at architecture and was interning at a local firm.

And Coby (Curly) had found his niche working for a lucrative moving company.

As shadows passed over the flora, Peter had the group start a campfire and pull out food for the evening while he reclined against a boulder. After a hearty dinner, conversation picked up.

Peter was distracted by the surrounding area for most of what John was saying, though he caught the last bit.

"*Every single lecture*," John thwacked his hand on his leg with each word. "My biology professor shows us a picture of an insect, and says to us, 'Aren't bugs voluptuous?'" He scrunched his brows. "I mean really, who says that about a bug?"

"An entomologist," Michael said with a teasing grin.

John shook his head. "Rightly so, Michael. But still, such a word for an insect."

"What's an entomologist?" Coby asked.

Peter sighed. Coby was always a little slow on the uptake. He was the only one who'd taken on the American accent—likely because he forgot how to speak British. He forgot everything.

"An entomologist is a scientist who studies insects," Thomas clarified in his know-it-all voice. "It would stand to reason that John's biology professor felt so strongly about them as to use such expressive terms in describing his feelings toward them because they are his life's study." He nodded once, satisfied with his comprehensive explanation. Being in law school had made him ridiculously verbose, and it irked Peter.

"Can we talk about something else?" Peter whined, clenching his hands on his thighs. "School is a tedious topic."

"Why *did* you quit classes at the local college?" Slater asked Peter with quizzical eyes. Though Slater's studies in music were his main focus, he'd found biology fascinating enough to minor in it. Another thing that irked Peter. Why did everyone have to keep learning things?

Peter scowled. "None of your business."

"You should've let Slater help you out with that, Peter," Coby nodded his head toward Slater. "He's a biology guru."

Peter released a sigh because Coby was right. *Oh well,* Peter thought. *I don't have to worry about that anymore.*

"Well, what do you want to talk about then, Peter?" Nick asked, irritation in his voice.

Peter surveyed the group, his smile lifting to one side while he leaned back against the boulder and put his hands behind his head. "Pranks," he said.

"Pranks?" Michael asked, sounding confused.

"Honestly, Peter." John groaned. "We're out here in this beautiful setting, we haven't seen each other in months, and you want to talk about pranks? As in, pranks we used to do in Neverland?" His response shouldn't have surprised Peter—he knew John thought talking about Neverland was not as worthwhile as talking about the present or the future.

But he cast an annoyed glance at John anyway. "*No.* Though we truly had some laughs at the expense of Hook and his ridiculous lot who had the audacity to call themselves *pirates.*"

"Yes, but we've moved on from all that," Thomas said as though addressing a child. "It was right fun to reminisce about when we first got here, but . . . ." He trailed off.

"But what?" Peter demanded, shooting a challenging glare at Thomas. He couldn't see the harm in talking about past escapades and laughing at the expense of Hook and his crew. The memories still amused him.

"But like Thomas said, we're past that, Peter." Coby shifted in his camping chair. If it had come from any of the other friends, Peter would have taken offense. But said in the innocence that came only from Coby, it gave his irritation the slightest poke.

Peter sat up and surveyed the group. "You've all 'moved on'?" he asked, using air quotes. "You all want to forget Neverland?" He couldn't fathom why any of them would want to forget. Neverland was home.

Michael leaned his elbows on his knees. "Not forget it, but just . . . not hang out in that train of thought over and over like we used to."

Peter pinched his mouth closed, scrunching his eyes and eyebrows in irritation.

"Suit yourselves," he said, suddenly relaxing his facial expression as though it didn't bother him in the slightest (though it bothered him quite a lot). "I wasn't referring to past pranks in *Neverland* anyway." Peter rolled his eyes like the thought was ridiculous. In reality, he loved talking about anything where he came out the strongest, smartest, or most heroic. Which was frequently the case with adventures in Neverland.

"Fair enough, Peter," Slater huffed, putting his face in one hand. "Tell us what kind of pranks you mean to talk about."

Peter looked around the group again to build suspense. "April first is coming up soon . . . ."

"What's that got to do with pranks?" the ever-innocent Coby asked with a bewildered expression.

Thomas cleared his throat. "In American culture, April first is referred to as 'April Fool's Day'—a day for tricks and mischief. I believe Peter intends to enact some sort of epic prank on an unsuspecting individual." He gave a satisfied nod at his assessment.

Peter scowled. Thomas stole all the glory from Peter's grand plan. He glowered at Thomas, who in turn looked surprised at Peter.

"What did I do?" Thomas asked, glancing around at everyone else.

"You stole his thunder," Nick rolled his eyes. "Peter never likes it when any of us know more than he does. Even though we're not in Neverland anymore and have all grown up, and such pettiness ought to be behind us." He shot Peter a disapproving look.

Peter shot one back at him. "It is, indeed, my aim to pull an epic prank on an unsuspecting individual, as Thomas so *helpfully* pointed out." He waved a hand toward Thomas. "However, how are any of you to know who that unsuspecting individual is?" His gaze roamed from person to person, his eyebrows raised.

"You mean to scare us with your stares, Peter?" Slater sat up and pointed his finger at Peter. "If some mischief befalls one of us in the next few days, we'll know *exactly* who to get back at. You've shown us all your cards—we've already caught you red-handed."

At the mention of "red-handed," Coby grinned. "Hey," he clapped his hands in a single loud smack. "Remember that time Wendy pretended to be a pirate named Red-Handed Jill?"

"I'd forgotten all about that. That was a right good joke of hers." Nick chuckled.

Coby's comment seemed to disperse the tension among the rest of the group, but Peter wanted to get back to their former topic.

"I thought we weren't talking of pranks from Neverland," he griped, tossing his hands up in irritation. He couldn't believe they had all come down on him for the idea of such a conversation, but it was well enough for someone else to bring it up.

Bunch of hypocrites, he thought.

"Hey John, Michael, how is Wendy?" Thomas asked, turning his attention to the Darling brothers. "It's been too long since we've seen her. I imagine she must have caught the attention of some bloke by now." He waggled his eyebrows. "Is she still a nurse at the children's clinic? Has that ever made you feel squeamish with the germs she might bring home? The fluids and substances that emerge from a sick body can be quite foul. Remember the time I came down with the stomach flu—"

"We get it, Thomas," Peter interrupted. Honestly, who spoke of bodily fluids in polite conversation? And the idea about Wendy dating someone? The thought filled him with angst.

Peter turned to John and Michael. "Is she seeing someone exclusively? I didn't get that impression when I saw her last. She still seems quite taken with me—as most women do."

John and Michael stared at Peter for a moment before John turned to Thomas. "To answer your questions, Wendy is doing well. She positively loves working with children. You know how she loves caring for people—she's always had such a way with nurturing others. But so far she hasn't brought home any dreadful disease, thankfully." He winked at Michael, who gave a half-smile back. "And as far as how her social life is going, she's not seeing anyone exclusively right now."

Silence hung in the air for a few breaths.

"Though she's been on several dates with different fellows," Michael added, looking up at John as though he'd forgotten that detail.

Peter frowned. *His* Wendy going out with other men? Wasn't he the only object of affection in her life? Not that they'd ever said that.

But wasn't there some sort of unspoken understanding between them? He'd been the one to help them after her parents' death, the one to take her on adventures, the one to save her from Hook and his miscreants time and again in Neverland. Didn't she owe him her admiration and commitment?

"You look confused, Peter," Coby said. "You okay?"

Peter softened his features at Coby's inquiry and pasted a smile on his face. "Of course," he lied.

He couldn't voice his true thoughts aloud without the others rebuking him on Wendy's behalf. They simply didn't understand that Wendy owed Peter her highest esteem since he'd done so much for her. He was completely justified in his reasoning. The rules were different for him.

"Well," Thomas said. "It's getting quite late in the evening. Or early in the morning, depending on how you look at it." He chuckled at his joke. "I, for one, ought to go to sleep soon. I've much to study tomorrow—"

"Alright, Thomas, we get it," Peter interrupted again. Hearing Thomas talk about school triggered insecurity in Peter, which he wouldn't tolerate.

Peter's agitation was tangible enough that everyone began to crawl into tents and sleeping bags without comment.

Except for Coby, who was ignorant of the tension. "Night, guys."

"Night, Coby," the rest of them said in unison.

~~~

Peter lay in his tent alone. He preferred solitude when sleeping, a habit formed in Neverland. He stewed in his thoughts, growing increasingly agitated. His friends had stressed the fact that they had all grown up and moved on.

Peter *had* grown up—he'd grown up quite nicely, if the reactions of the ladies had anything to say about it. *Which they did*, he smiled smugly. He felt he'd grown up better-looking than any of them. And stronger too. He stayed physically active. Thomas was becoming as soft as a ball of dough in law school. Yes, Peter was better than the others.

As his musings turned to Wendy, his delight wilted. He hadn't retained his position on her pedestal of importance like he thought he should. He needed to correct that. Or chasten her for it. He smiled roguishly.

Yes, he would teach her a lesson. He would teach her that he was still the only hero in her life.

She would be the unsuspecting individual who would be the brunt of his April Fool's prank. He extended his hands behind his head and closed his eyes, his lips widening in an impish grin.

I'll show her.

CHAPTER FIVE

B reaking out of one's comfort zone is often intimidating. Such was the case for Wendy as she thought about the fencing class for that evening.

She turned off the nurse's station computer for the day, satisfied with her work. Interacting with children always brought her joy, though doing so all day left her exhausted.

"You're still here, amiga?" a Latina voice said from around the corner.

Wendy startled. "Karmen," she exhaled. "You truly ought to make your presence known before speaking."

Karmen chuckled. "And you truly ought to be getting ready by now."

"Someone left the computer on."

Karmen twirled her deep brown hair with her finger while popping a gum bubble. "And?"

"You know that's against policy. I didn't want someone to get in trouble."

"Always thinking of others," Karmen teased. "But really, go home and get ready. I don't want to do this class alone."

Wendy pulled her bag out of her designated drawer and followed Karmen out the clinic doors. "I still don't understand why you need me there."

"Girls travel in packs, remember? Or in our case, pairs. Anyway, I hear the fencing teacher is ridiculously sexy and I don't want to go by myself in case I faint from his hotness or from exercise or both, because if I do, I'll need you to drive me home—"

"Point taken." Wendy stopped her friend's rambling with an amused expression.

Karmen squealed as she unlocked her car. "I can't wait to see this man. I hear he has the most gorgeous blue eyes and the sexiest accent. Maybe we can get his number."

"Like last week when you tried to get the number for the policeman that pulled you over?"

"Psh. Don't bring that up. My point is, we're going to get this man's attention or die trying."

"I'd rather not die," Wendy teased while folding her arms and leaning against Karmen's car.

"Okay, so no dying. But it'll still be fun."

Wendy regarded her one and only female friend. Befriending girls had never come easy to Wendy—even in London. But Karmen was a rare unassuming breed. She met her tall South American friend in their nursing program, and they were fortunate enough to find work together at the pediatric clinic. Friday night outings had become their tradition, and the Friday night fencing class would be their activity for the next eight weeks.

Wendy smirked. "I'll be ready on time, and we will conquer this together."

"Si, we will be victoriosas." Karmen bit her lower lip and smiled. "Maybe he'll ask one of us out."

"That's ridiculous. What if he's already dating someone, or married?"

"What if he isn't?" Karmen challenged. "Between the two of us, this man won't know what hit him. Unless we hit him with one of those fencing sticks, because, you know, he'll see it."

Wendy shook her head and waved goodbye to Karmen before heading to her car, her mind mulling over the idea of a man's serious interest directed at her.

"Absurd," she muttered, then started her car.

She pulled up to a stoplight and flicked on her turn signal to go left. The steady beat reminded her of the dreaded crocodile in Neverland, with the constant ticking emanating from its body. And the thought of the crocodile turned her thoughts to Captain Hook, who was usually on the lookout for the large, ugly beast who wanted to finish him off.

What sort of thing does a villain do without a hero to contend with? she wondered.

With Peter gone from Neverland, would Hook be content with his life? No more of Peter's shenanigans to pester the pirates, no more Peter playing the hero, no more ambushing Hook. Peter had saved Wendy from plenty of Hook's retaliations against Peter's mischief. Maybe the pirates could finally sail away from Neverland and live out their lives in peace.

She'd felt sympathy for Hook before they left for Reality. Peter was genuinely provoking, and Hook had been his favorite target. Ever since she'd grown up, Wendy realized how childish Peter's intrigues with the

35

pirates were. Why couldn't he just leave them alone? What was there to prove? What had Captain Hook done to make Peter harass him?

Hook had been several years older than her when Peter first took her to Neverland. But when she and her brothers returned after their parents' death, time in the real world had caught her up to his twenty-something age. She remembered feeling herself blush in his presence the first time they encountered the pirates after their return. Her mature self could appreciate what her child self hadn't before: his eyes the color of forget-me-not flowers, dark hair, tall stature, chiseled form, his commanding presence, and a maturity that Peter had lacked—and still did. Her heart rate sped up as a memory surfaced.

Days before convincing Peter to leave Neverland, Wendy had been captured by the pirates to lure Peter to them. When they brought her to Captain Hook, Wendy realized that rather than being terrified, she was entranced by his appearance. His broad shoulders stretched his uniform, and she'd imagined the muscles that filled it out. His hair was windswept, though pulled to a low ponytail, like something from a gothic novel.

The only thing more mesmerizing than his forget-me-not blue eyes was the dashing smirk on his lips. She couldn't pull her eyes away from them. She'd even let her mind wander to what his lips would feel like on hers. And when she finally lifted her eyes to his face, she caught him staring at her lips too. Her mind swam with euphoria before remembering she'd been taken as a hostage and not because the captain wanted her in that way.

Cars honked behind Wendy, bringing her out of her memory to see the green traffic light. She quickly moved her car forward and shook her head. Hook was a villain, and he was in the past. Peter was in the present. And Peter was the hero. Sort of. Maybe?

But what kind of hero treated Wendy the way Peter treated her—like some chum or convenient sidekick? As though she was supposed to sit on a shelf and wait for him to pull her down to admire him when he needed an ego boost. Ogling those women at their last rendezvous hadn't been the first time Peter ignored Wendy in favor of staring at a pretty girl in his line of sight. That wasn't heroic.

Her musings carried her all the way home. She expected to see John and Michael in the front room, where she usually found them either studying or playing video games. ("It's a brain break," John often justified.)

Her brows knit in confusion as she took in the empty room and quiet home.

"Oh, that's right," she said aloud as she remembered. "Camping trip." She likely wouldn't see them until tomorrow afternoon, which meant she had the place to herself.

"Which means," she wiggled her fingers, "that I can listen to whatever music I want as loud as I like." She pulled out her phone and set her music app to her favorite "Wendy's Mix" playlist and hit Play. She moved to the beat of Taylor Swift while heading up the stairs to get ready for class before Karmen picked her up.

CHAPTER SIX

"I didn't know they taught so many things here," Wendy said to Karmen as they pulled up to the martial arts studio. A sign on the front window displayed a myriad of classes—martial arts, yoga, HIIT fitness, self-defense, and fencing.

"Let's get this hottie party started." Karmen grinned as they entered the building.

Wendy elbowed her friend. "He might hear you," she whispered.

"Where's your sense of adventure, chica?" Karmen whispered back.

I left it in Neverland, Wendy thought wryly.

They spotted a set of lockers to their immediate left for personal belongings. They stored their bags there before turning to take in the rest of the studio. A floor-to-ceiling set of mirrors lined the far side of the room, while benches ran perpendicular to the mirrors. Their classmates sat on the benches, some in groups, some alone.

A cluster of women her age took up a large portion of the benches on the left, clad in the latest activewear, their hair and makeup in line with the current trends.

Wendy took in her own attire—a fitted T-shirt and sweatpants—and felt her confidence wilt.

"Perhaps I'm a bit underdressed," she told Karmen.

Karmen turned Wendy to face her and took her by the shoulders. "You're excelente just as you are. And you're gonna crush those Lulu Lemonheads with your skills."

Wendy seriously doubted her skills would come back quickly. It had been several years since she'd even seen a sword, let alone used one. She, her brothers, Peter, and the Lost Boys had sword fights so many times—playing with each other, fighting the pirates, battling other dangers. Would the knowledge, skills, and abilities return?

Karmen drank a few gulps from her water bottle, reminding Wendy she'd left hers in her locker. "I'll be right back."

"Okay, but hurry. I think he's coming out soon." Karmen nodded to the back offices.

Wendy fumbled with the locker door, which seemed reluctant to open for her. She gave it a final tug, and it flew open. She sighed and pulled the water bottle out before shoving the door closed. Still facing the lockers, she had the bottle halfway to her mouth when the instructor arrived.

"Welcome to Fencing. My name is Evan," he said.

Wendy's eyes went wide—she knew that voice. That voice had given her pleasant chills and set her heart pounding the last time she'd heard it.

"We'll begin today by practicing a few basics and becoming familiar with the terms," he continued. "Has anyone ever used..." His voice trailed off.

Wendy turned toward the instructor, only to find him staring at her with his mouth ajar.

He wore a dark gray, form-fitting cap sleeve tank top (which displayed his arm and shoulder muscles to perfection) and black athletic pants. His dark hair was tied back in a low ponytail. He had familiar deep blue eyes; a tall, lean form; a commanding presence; and his right hand was missing. He looked exactly like ...

"Hook," Wendy breathed out as her pulse quickened in a familiar way.

How, and why, was Captain Hook in Reality?

~~~

Evan spoke to the class and surveyed the students. When the woman at the lockers faced him, he stopped. He recognized her long honey-colored hair, her delicate facial features, her lovely blue eyes, and her regal stature. When she spoke, he knew for certain who she was.

"Hook." It was barely a whisper.

Intelligent thought left his brain. "Wendy?"

Her slack-jaw expression likely mirrored his own. What was she doing here? Not that he was unhappy to see her. But he never thought he would see her here.

"Um," he said while coming back to the present. He was supposed to be teaching, not staring at her. "Have any of you ever used a sword?"

Wendy tentatively raised her hand in answer to Evan's question. "I have. Sir."

He smirked. Of course she'd used a sword before. He'd seen her in action plenty of times to know how adept she was with one. And how good she looked while using one.

Focus, Roberts, he told himself, though memories of Wendy in action sent his heart thumping.

Wendy cleared her throat. "But it's been some time since I've used one."

"Well then, Miss Wendy, please step forward and let us see how much you remember." Evan grinned wickedly. Oh, to spar with Wendy again. Memories of past fights with her in Neverland surfaced. He remembered how her body moved, how her hair fell out of its placement, and the set of her lips as they clashed swords again and again.

He went to the far side of the room, picked up two fencing foils with his left hand, slipped two masks onto his right arm, then strode back to the front of the room.

Wendy approached him, her chin lifted. Evan tossed one of the foils to her and she caught it while still looking at him. Then he tossed her a mask, which she also caught while not breaking eye contact with him. They faced each other, sizing one another up, then they slipped the masks over their heads.

Evan moved into position, his foil pointed toward Wendy, his heart rate in high gear. "En garde, Miss Wendy." He gave her a mischievous smile. She set her mouth in determination.

Just like old times.

CHAPTER SEVEN

Wendy certainly looked forward to a shower that night with all the sweat covering her body. She wasn't the only one—all the students were sweating by the end of class. Though Wendy's perspiration came from more than just physical activity. Simply being around Hook set her senses on fire.

Students filed out, and Wendy realized Karmen was missing. She pulled her bag out of the locker and checked her phone.

Karmen: *Brb. Have fun with the instructor.*

The text was followed by a wink emoji. Blast it—had Karmen done this on purpose? She began to text Karmen an irritated message, then sensed someone behind her. She took a deep inhale and let it out slowly as she turned around. She stared at a man's tight chest in a dark gray shirt and had to tilt her head up to see the face that went with it.

"Miss Darling," Hook/Evan gave a polite nod, his hands in his pockets.

Had the heater kicked on? The room was suddenly blazing hot. Wendy blinked twice.

"Sir," she said as she stared into his hypnotic eyes. No, she couldn't let herself go there. "Or Evan. Is that what you call yourself here?" She crossed her arms over her chest to quell the butterflies in her stomach.

"Yes, Miss Darling," He smiled lopsidedly. "My real name is Evander, or Evan. It's who I was before 'Captain Hook,'" he used air quotes with his left hand, "and it's who I am again."

Wendy narrowed her eyes in confusion. "Then why were you called Hook in," she dropped her voice to a whisper, "Neverland?"

He smiled at the whispered word. She knew it was unnecessary as they were the only ones in the building, but she wasn't going to say Neverland aloud so anyone could overhear.

"I never gave myself that name, Miss Darling—"

"It's just Wendy, if you please." She waved the formality out of the way. "I'm not a little girl anymore."

He hitched an eyebrow as his gaze took her in. "No, you certainly aren't."

The intensity in his eyes sent Wendy's heart flying faster than she'd ever flown by air.

"Very well then, just Wendy," Evan smirked. "If you please, call me Evan. I was dubbed 'Captain Hook' by Peter after he disposed of my hand. I put a hook there to replace what he'd taken." He waved his arm slightly before dropping it back down to his side.

Wendy had just been thinking of the incident with Peter, and Hook's hand—Evan's hand. Realizing that this man before her was more than just a pirate captain—that he had a real name—opened a curtain to a window in her mind she hadn't known was there before.

But this man was an enemy.

43

"Wait—how did you get here?" Wendy asked in alarm, suddenly unfolding her arms and clenching her hands by her sides. Evan opened his mouth to answer but Wendy quickly continued her interrogation before he could form any words.

"Did you follow us? Were you planning to harm us—to exact your revenge on Peter for good? There's no magic here. He's as mortal as anyone in the real world."

She tapped her finger on her leg and looked at the floor. "Yes, that must be it," she muttered. "He must've followed us, knowing Peter would have no magic, couldn't fly away. Now he's here to—" She broke off her rambling and glared at Evan, pointing an accusing finger at him. "Whatever it is you've come to do, just leave all of us alone."

She headed for the door, irritated that Karmen would leave her here. She'd get a ride share and go home.

But Evan had her by the arm before she made it two steps away. She turned and stared at his hand on her arm. Her skin tingled at his touch.

Then her eyes lifted to Evan's pleading face.

Wendy took a deep breath. *I haven't given him a chance to answer my questions.* Her emotions faded from anger to contrition.

"I'm sorry for judging you. But given what you are, how can I not feel threatened by your presence here?"

Evan released his grip on her, then crossed his arms over his solid chest. Wendy felt her neck heat up as she took in the definition of his arms.

Evan regarded her with sternness for a few moments. "And just what am I, Miss Darling?"

"You're the villain. Sir." Wendy tilted her chin up and scowled while crossing her arms across her chest, refusing to be intimidated by him.

44

Evan gave a half-smile, and her heart jumped to her throat. This was Hook's signature smile—the one he used whenever he had the upper hand in a situation. It was just as disarming here as it was there. The room seemed to tilt, and Wendy blinked several times before shaking her head to clear her thoughts.

Evan tilted his chin down and narrowed his eyes at her, still smiling. "Let me ask you something, Miss Darling."

Wendy narrowed her eyes at him. "Ask away, sir."

"Are you free this evening?"

"What?" Wendy pulled her head back, blinking in surprise.

"I thought we might continue our conversation," Evan said. "Unless you'd rather verbally spar elsewhere." He looked around the studio and back at her.

Wendy stood straight, her expression serious. "I have no other plans tonight, but what makes you think I'd like to spend the rest of the evening with you, sir?"

He straightened, a teasing smile tugging at his lips. "We can do away with the formalities, Wendy. We aren't in," he leaned in and dramatically whispered, "Neverland." He went back to normal volume. "And seeing that your ride has fled, might I offer you a ride home?"

Wendy cocked her head. "I'm not showing *you* where I live."

He threw his head back and laughed. The sound pierced her sternum and sent butterflies fluttering in her stomach.

His expression turned from levity to sobriety. "May I at least answer your questions and have you listen without judgment?" His eyes turned down and to the side while he rubbed the back of his neck briefly. He returned his gaze to her, waiting for an answer.

"Yes. I suppose."

"How could you leave me there for two hours?" Wendy asked Karmen with a scowl on their way home.

"I seriously got lost. I promise." Karmen navigated the streets leading home. "I thought I set the app to take me to that new health food store, and it took me across town by the lake. Do you know how many flies are down there? They were all over the car."

"Karmen," Wendy interrupted. She put her hand on the side of her face. "I know you meant well, but never do that again."

Karmen put up two fingers. "Scout's honor."

Wendy adjusted the gesture to include three fingers. "My brothers are actual Boy Scouts, and this is how you do it."

Karmen waved her hand. "Okay, so I won't do that again, and you forgive me." She turned her unsure eyes to Wendy, who rolled her eyes but smiled. Karmen's face relaxed as she smiled back. "Tell me about Evan."

Wendy sighed. "Where to start?"

"Somehow, you knew him already," Karmen accused. "And you didn't tell me."

"I didn't know his name was Evan."

"Si, you called him Hook." Karmen slanted an eyebrow in reprimand. "The man is missing a hand. That was kinda low."

"That's not what I meant. It's just what he was called before."

"You guys sparred like you've done that before." Karmen raised her eyebrows.

"We have." Wendy's chest flamed as she replayed their fencing match in her mind. She'd lost. It wasn't her fault, though. That smirk on his lips kept bringing up thoughts of kissing him.

"And ..." Karmen prompted.

"Maybe I can tell you more about him another time. It was a shock to see him again, and we're already here." She nodded to her townhome.

"Fine." Karmen sighed. "But you'll tell me more on Monday?"

"Yes, and I'll even bring those cinnamon donuts you love."

Karmen squealed. "This is why you're the favorita of the clinic." Her eyes landed on Wendy's front door. "Are your brothers home?"

"No, they're on a campout tonight."

Karman nodded absently. "Bien. Adios, mi amiga." She then drove down the street, leaving Wendy wondering why Karmen would ask about John and Michael.

∽

After showering, Wendy lay in her bed in her pajamas, thinking about her conversation with Evan.

"Why are you here?" she'd asked him as they sat on a bench after class.

"My intentions are pure." He'd lifted his left hand. "You remember your arguments with Peter about leaving Neverland? He wasn't the only one you convinced." He leaned against the wall and crossed his arms. "I'd grown tired of piracy and the inane escapades with Peter. I wanted a new start."

Wendy had paused while allowing that information to settle in her mind. "What did you do when you got here?"

Evan shrugged. "I found honest work, a place to live, and took action to break poor habits."

"Has it worked?"

He turned his head to her. "Did you hear me swear or yell at all tonight?"

"No."

"Did you see me drunk, or barking orders at anyone?"

Wendy nodded. "Very well. Point taken." She couldn't help but follow up with, "What about your social situation?"

He quirked an eyebrow in question.

"Have you any friends? Girlfriends?" She immediately regretted asking—it was none of her business.

"I've met several people."

Wendy turned her head to the window then, watching cars pass. She pictured Evan with another woman and her chest tightened. Her fingers fidgeted, playing with her nails and tapping on her leg. "Just so," she squeaked out.

"What does it matter to you?" Evan asked, leaning into her line of sight.

Wendy shrugged. "It doesn't."

"Hm." Evan leaned against the wall again.

Wendy huffed, eager to move to different topics. "How did you get here? Pixie dust? Did Tinkerbell help you?"

"No. I stowed away on the ship."

Wendy turned to him. "Where? How? None of us saw you."

"I'm a former pirate, Wendy. I can be stealthy when needed. I left my crew, snuck off my ship, and hid in the *Jolly Roger*. The hull had plenty of hiding places. Though I admit it was quite jarring down there with all the barrels when the ship crash-landed."

The sound of a dog barking outside Wendy's bedroom window broke her free from the memory of her conversation with Evan. And what a rather enlightening conversation it was. He was no longer the pirate captain from Neverland. He had a real name, a job, a life.

She frowned. A life that might include a girlfriend. What bothered her about that was that it actually *bothered* her thinking of him with another woman.

Blast it, Wendy. There's no use becoming jealous over someone you've no chance with.

She could still dream, though. She dreamed of him several times that night, dancing in his arms.

She woke the next morning disoriented. What would she do now? She could stop going to class with Karmen and move on from any thoughts of Evan. She could return and torture herself while longing for something that might not be. Perhaps she could ask John and Michael . . .

No, that would be unwise. As her brothers, they could become overprotective and advise her to stay away from Evan. They might not believe him to be the changed man he explained to her last night.

What about Peter—should he know about Hook? I mean, Evan? No, if John and Michael could become defensive, then Peter would definitely do something rash and regrettable.

Wendy realized that Peter hadn't come to fencing class like he said he would.

Like he said he might. *He probably forgot about it when he went on the campout.*

Her stomach growled and she checked the time on her phone. Nearly noon.

As she made her way downstairs, she heard a key scratch the doorknob, and a moment later the front door swung open with John standing in the doorway. "We're ho-ome!" came John's voice with a singsongy lilt. He and Michael brought in their bags and gear, setting them on the floor with a loud thump.

"How was your weekend, Wendy?" John asked. "We had a lovely time in the woods."

Wendy reached to bring her brothers in for a hug before backing away. "Yes, it smells as though you did," she teased.

"It's true," John agreed. "Campfire and nature have a potent scent. We'll just get washed up then."

Her brothers went down the hall to their shared room and bathroom, and Wendy went to the kitchen to make lunch.

How was she going to keep Evan a secret? *Should* she keep Evan a secret? Yes, at least for now. What her brothers didn't know wouldn't bother them.

CHAPTER EIGHT

What a wasted weekend, Peter thought at home after the campout. *No one cared what I had to say. Everyone's grown up and left me behind. Idiots.*

He'd always been the leader of the group, but since landing here, the Lost Boys had come into their own and depended less and less on his guidance.

It's insulting. Maybe if they don't need me anymore, I don't need them anymore. After all I've done for them, you'd think they'd still respect my position. They said they've grown up. Well, they aren't growing up to be very respectful adults now, are they? Bunch of self-important, ungrateful friends.

He arrived late for work, but punctuality had never been his forte. His arms were full of camping gear anyway. He hated making several trips to get anything from one place to another. He stored away the items in their respective places in the storage room, then headed to the front desk to take calls and make appointments.

Outdoor Adventure Trek was always busy on the weekends. Today was no exception— groups young and old alike came and went on guided hikes. He envied the trek guides, wishing it could be him taking clients out. Instead, he ran the front desk.

Before he knew it, closing time rolled around and customers trickled out. The guides stored their gear, and everyone set to work tidying up for the day.

Except Peter—tidying up wasn't his favorite. He slid into the back room where he knew he'd find Tessa and Jane, the female guides, shelving their supplies away.

Tessa turned to him, her signature smile brightening as it always did when he was nearby. "Hey Peter. What'd you do this weekend?"

"I went camping with some old friends. Though it wasn't as much fun as I anticipated." He turned his eyes to the ground, frowning. "Seems my friends don't need me as much as they used to."

"What happened?" Jane asked as she paused her work. Peter felt a sense of accomplishment at her sympathy.

"I guess they've moved on from me." He shook his head sadly. "Whenever I tried to contribute to the conversation, someone would brush off my ideas and opinions. Like I don't matter."

"That's a terrible feeling," Tessa said, then frowned. "Friends shouldn't treat each other that way. But *we're* your friends." She gestured to herself and Jane, who nodded.

Ah, Tessa. Ever the peacemaker and problem-solver.

Peter nodded with pretend humility. "What will you do for the rest of the weekend, ladies?" He hoped he could squeeze his way into one of their plans.

Tessa shrugged her shoulder and brushed her brown hair over it. "Nothing too exciting. Not like Jane." She smiled at her friend.

Peter turned to Jane. "What mighty adventure do you have planned?"

Jane blushed— a reaction Peter induced in many women. A reaction that never failed to please him. "I'm going with a few friends to Vegas. Just a quick girls' trip. We'll probably see a show and eat too much."

Peter frowned theatrically. "And you'll leave me behind?"

Jane giggled. "No guys allowed. Besides, Tessa's free tonight."

"She's not going with you?" he asked.

"The Las Vegas Strip is the last place you'd ever find Tessa," Jane said, still smiling at her friend. "Her values go in a different direction."

Tessa nodded unapologetically. "It's true."

"Then what are your plans?" Peter asked her.

"I'm going to a girl's night with my roommates." Peter turned pleading eyes to her, and she grinned. "But I suppose they wouldn't mind if you come."

"Even if it's bending the rules?" Peter asked with a raised eyebrow. "You tend to stick to the rules, Tess."

Tessa's cheeks pinked. "Just Tessa. You'll behave, won't you?"

Peter straightened. "Of course. I'm always a perfect gentleman."

Jane headed to the door. "I gotta get going."

"You're sure your roommates won't mind?" Peter asked once they were alone.

Tessa smiled platonically. "My roommates love British accents and red hair, and you have both. You'll be a hit. Besides, it's just a movie and some take-out. You can't get into much trouble with that."

"Or can I?" Peter turned his smolder on her. Her neck turned red, and her lips parted. Just the reaction he'd meant to produce to tease her. He stepped toward her, this rule-following straight-arrow. Her breathing picked up as he neared her.

She shook her head from her trance and giggled. "You're nothing but trouble, Peter."

"Guilty as charged." He winked. Let her think his advances were playful. He meant to see how many rules he could get her to bend tonight. What a fun game that would be.

Maybe this weekend won't turn out so bad after all, he thought with satisfaction.

CHAPTER NINE

Wendy was in Evan's thoughts the entire weekend.

But Monday morning came bright and early, and with it, a day's worth of moving jobs to tackle. Evan was checking the moving van to prepare for departure when Coby arrived.

"Hey Evan," Coby said.

Evan glanced at his coworker from the vertical sliding door he was double-checking. "I hope you had breakfast because there's a lot to move today. You'll need the energy."

"It's the most important meal of the day," Coby said, smiling. "I wouldn't miss it."

Evan sat in the driver's seat, making sure all things were in order in the cab. Coby swung up into the passenger seat and pulled up their schedule on his phone.

"Let's roll," he said.

Evan paused, the keys nearly to the ignition, before noticing Coby's incomplete position. He raised his eyebrows, nodding his head at Coby's unfastened seatbelt. "Aren't you forgetting something?"

"What?" Coby asked, bewildered. He looked around his seat, down at the floor, then out the window.

Evan chuckled. "Your seatbelt." He nodded to it again. "Let's not attract police attention and get pulled over again."

"So just drive the speed limit," Coby joked as he buckled up.

Evan started the engine and shook his head, smiling.

"What'd you do this weekend?" Coby asked as they rolled out onto the street.

Evan's thoughts immediately went to Wendy, as they had all weekend. Sparring with her again and seeing the sheen of sweat on her forehead had driven him mad with longing. Then she'd accused him of nefarious intentions by following them to Reality. It made sense, as he'd been their enemy. But she'd given him the chance to explain himself. Now the question was whether she'd return to class on Friday.

He must have been quiet for too long.

"That bad, huh?" Coby prodded.

"No, sorry." Evan gave his head a small shake. "It was an interesting weekend. I ran into an old friend. We were able to catch up—it's been a few years."

"Was your friend at the class? How did that go?" Coby asked while holding his seatbelt strap.

"Class went well." Evan took a deep breath and drew it out slowly. "And yes, my friend was there. We showed everyone a few fencing techniques." He shifted in his seat, not yet comfortable talking about Wendy as he was still processing his interaction with her. "What did you do this weekend?"

"Went camping with some old friends. Good times." He smiled. "Had some laughs, ate some food, slept in the cold. It gets *super* cold in the woods at night. I wasn't in a tent."

"You mean you didn't *have* a tent, or you chose not to sleep in one?"

"Oh, I chose not to. I like seeing the stars." Coby shrugged. "But if I do that again, I'm bringing a beanie to keep my head warm." His body shuddered involuntarily. "It was so freaking cold."

"Not just cold, but 'freaking cold.' That must be frigid indeed."

Coby swatted Evan's side, then pulled up their schedule for the day. "Is the first job an office move? This doesn't look like a house address."

"Yes, just moving from one office to another. It shouldn't take too long, and they're both on the ground floor."

"Nice," Coby said while doing a fist bump with Evan.

They made quick work of the first two jobs. The extra time afforded them the opportunity to stop for lunch early and eat in the moving van.

Evan turned to Coby. "Where are your camping friends from? Do they live nearby?"

"We all live around here," Coby answered, circling his hand in the air and tilting his head side to side. "Well, here-ish. Some are in school, some are working. One guy works for some outdoors company. That's where we get most of our camping gear. He gets to use it for free sometimes."

Coby paused in thought for a moment. "Some brothers in the group have a sister, but she didn't come. She usually doesn't since it's not really her thing now. I wish I could take her out on a date, but we're all like brothers to her. Except for the one guy who works at the outdoors place. I think she's had a thing for him for a while."

Coby paused again. "Hey, maybe I could set you up with her." His face lit up and he turned to face Evan.

"I thought you said she was interested in one of your other friends," Evan countered, lifting his eyebrows.

"Yeah, but he's been stringing her along forever. Like he can't decide if he wants to go for it or not." Coby faced front and seemed lost in thought. Then his eyes widened. "I better watch my back this week. My friend hinted at some kind of prank for April Pools." He shook his head. "I hate getting wet."

"Do you mean 'April Fools'?" Evan asked, hiding a grin at Coby's innocent misunderstanding.

Coby smiled good-naturedly. "Yeah, that. Anyway, the guy has pulled some serious pranks in the past. He doesn't really think before he acts. But then again, I don't really think before I talk."

Evan looked over at his friend. "You're a good sort, Coby. Give yourself some credit."

Coby nodded. "I know. I'm just slower than most people, but I'm okay with it." He looked at the clock on the dashboard. "We better get going again. Where's the next place?"

That night after work, Evan thought back on his conversation with Coby. He hoped his guileless friend wouldn't be the target of someone's prank—he was a genuinely good person who didn't deserve to be the brunt of a trick.

He also hoped Coby wouldn't bring up the idea of setting him up on a date again. Because now that Wendy had reentered his life, he doubted any other woman could drive her from his mind. Or his heart.

CHAPTER TEN

Monday at the clinic had Wendy smiling throughout the day. The doctors, nurses, and staff took advantage of April Fool's Day jokes.

Someone had changed all the staff monitors to a large picture of a pediatrician's face. Karmen had a dad joke ready for each grade-school age patient that came in that day. (Oh, the eye rolling and groans the parents gave.) The pediatricians had covered the nurse's station in sticky notes. And on went the silliness throughout the workday.

"Hey amiga," Karmen said as she and Wendy left the clinic. "Why do seagulls live by the sea?"

"Not another one," Wendy laughed.

"Because if they lived by the bay, they'd be bay-gulls. You know, like bagels?"

Wendy groaned. "I think that was the worst one of the day."

Karmen held up her phone. "I got more."

"Next year," Wendy said while unlocking her car.

"Say hi to your bros for me," Karmen called as she walked away.

At home that night, Wendy, John, and Michael had been invited by their new neighbors to play games. The neighbor's daughter, Emily, had classes with Michael at the high school, and the parents had texted Wendy, eager to know the Darling siblings better.

Michael and Emily made a wicked team during charades and sat next to each other while the group played Uno. Wendy noticed the two sharing looks and nudging each other. She found herself smiling at the friendship unfolding between them.

John, however, was oblivious to Alexis, Emily's older sister who was near his age. Each smile Alexis gave him went unnoticed. Her offer to partner with him was met with, "No, Wendy's better at this game. I'll partner with her." And when she offered him a donut at the end, John focused more on the donut than on her.

The poor girl was no match for John's clueless nature. In his defense, donuts were his favorite, and Wendy supposed not even a burning building could take his attention away when he had a donut in his midst.

The Darlings bid their neighbors a good night, then set off down the sidewalk to their townhome. Wendy felt a hand on her arm after she'd gone ten steps.

She turned to see Michael, with Emily next to him. "What're you two doing?" she asked.

"Emily says she can help me with the math assignment," he explained while glancing at his friend.

"I suppose that's alright," Wendy answered, her eyes darting between the two. "Just be home by curfew."

"I always am," Michael answered before heading to Emily's again.

"Are you coming, Wendy?" John called from their front door.

The evening air held a pleasant scent that only springtime supplied. Birds called from tree to tree, their tiny voices playing back and forth in the fading daylight. "I think I'll go for a walk."

"Do you want me to come?" John asked in a way that told Wendy he hoped she would decline his offer.

"No, I'll be alright on my own." She headed down the sidewalk at a relaxed pace, taking in the budding flowers of yellow, pink, and purple. She wondered why she didn't do this more often. Perhaps evening walks could be an addition to her daily routine. The combination of fresh air, exercise, and lovely flowers could benefit her soul.

She turned the corner and went down the next block of the neighborhood. A few people walked their dogs, several joggers passed by, and at one point a squirrel darted up a tree. Wendy paused to take in an assortment of tulips and daffodils in various colors in someone's front yard. She bent down to inhale the scent, sighing satisfactorily afterward. Yes, evening walks were a definite must.

She stood to continue her stroll, and her head was immediately swarmed by a cloud of gnats. She gasped, accidentally inhaling some of the nasty invaders. Her arms and hands swatted the tiny flies in vain. She remembered hearing somewhere that gnats were drawn to body heat, so she began to run down the sidewalk to outdistance them. She ran the rest of the block, then turned the next corner and ran that entire block. When she reached the final corner that would take her home, she slowed to her original pace to catch her breath. She hadn't gone that fast since fleeing from dangers in Neverland. She coughed a few more times to rid her throat of the irritation the inhaled gnats had caused. She'd be more careful during her future evening walks to avoid insects as much as possible.

She sighed in relief as her townhome came into view. Her hand fumbled in her pocket to retrieve her keys as she approached the front steps. She had her key out and ready to insert into the lock before she noticed an unwelcome addition to the front porch.

Wendy's hand flew to her mouth to keep from screaming. A rattlesnake lay coiled on the welcome mat, eyeing her warily. Wendy's breathing became shallow beneath her hand and her mind went blank in her panic. She stepped backward and tripped down the stairs, scraping her hands on the sidewalk.

The motion alerted the snake, which slithered off the mat. Wendy rolled away and sat up at the bottom of the stairs, her eyes in a staring match with the snake's. She knew rattlesnakes weren't unheard of in their area, but she'd never seen one in person. And she'd never anticipated one guarding her front porch. Its forked tongue slipped in and out of its mouth as the legless body approached the top step and its head hovered above the next stair. Wendy pulled back in automatic fear, which startled the snake. It coiled up, all except for the end of its tail, which began to vibrate and rattle.

She was going to die. The snake would strike, bite her, inject its venom, and then her insides would turn to mush, and she would expire slowly, agonizingly. All because she hadn't seen the snake in time. Who would provide for her brothers? What would happen to them? How much would dying hurt? And who would tell Evan? That last thought jolted her consciousness.

Then spots collected in the corners of her vision, and just before her strength gave away, a person appeared in her periphery to catch her as she passed out.

Chapter Eleven

Wendy awoke to the sight of a car's interior. Momentarily groggy, she didn't think herself in any potential danger.

I'm lying in the front seat of someone's car, her mind registered suddenly.

She sat up and her forehead collided with someone else's. Former training from Neverland had her fist immediately aiming for the person's jaw, but a swift hand caught her wrist.

"Peter?"

His signature cocky grin appeared. "Thought you could hit me, hm?"

"You've always had lightning reflexes," Wendy conceded while straightening. "What am I doing in your car?"

"I caught you as you passed out and carried you away from that rattlesnake."

A chill ran up Wendy's spine as she remembered the immediate danger she'd been in and the way the snake made its way toward her. She could still hear the rattle of its tail.

Peter put his hand on her arm and ducked his head to catch her eye. "You're safe now, Wendy. I took care of the snake. Nasty fight it put up too. It nearly got me." He showed her a spot on his arm where a couple scrapes burned an angry shade of red.

Wendy's hand went to her mouth. He'd done that for her? She thought he'd been impartial to her feelings and didn't care for her at all. But this—this was heroic.

She met his eyes, their corners crinkled as he smiled. Her eyes welled with tears, and Peter supplied a tissue for her to dab the wetness away. "Thank you," she muttered.

He gave her arm a gentle squeeze. "Friends care for each other. I'm just grateful I happened to pass by at the right moment."

"So am I." Wendy glanced out the darkened window. "What time is it?"

Peter checked his phone. "It's nearly ten."

"John and Michael must be sick with worry." She'd left her phone at home for game night and didn't think to bring it with her on her walk. "Can you take me home?"

Peter nodded and they drove away, being only a few blocks away from her home.

Peter's proximity to her house made Wendy wonder. "What brought you out here tonight? You're not often in our neighbor-hood." She hoped she didn't sound ungrateful for his sparse appear-ance at their home after he'd just saved her from the snake.

He shrugged. "I just had a feeling I needed to be here tonight." He then parked next to the curb in front of their townhouse and got out of the car, meeting Wendy at the front step.

"Do you want to come in?" Wendy asked, assuming he did, since he came up to the porch.

"I want to see you safely inside," Peter answered.

John and Michael were sitting on the couch, John's phone next to his ear. "Never mind, Officer. She's here—we found her." He hung up as he and Michael jumped up from the couch.

"Wendy, what on earth happened?" John exclaimed.

Peter guided Wendy to the couch and sat next to her.

Maybe Peter is still a hero after all.

"I went on a walk and when I got back there was a rattlesnake on the porch."

Her brother's eyes widened. "A rattlesnake? Here?" John searched the room as though a snake might show up out of nowhere.

Michael came over with a damp cloth and placed it on her forehead. "Your face is flushed. This should help cool it off."

I must look awful.

"I caught her just before she passed out," Peter filled in. "Then I carried her to my car and took care of the snake."

Wendy shivered. "Let's not say that word for the rest of the night." Why did she have to be afraid of snakes? Why not something like sharks that lived far away?

"You're safe now," Peter reassured her. "You're home and the thing is gone." He finished with a teasing smirk, pulling a smile out of Wendy. The shift in her facial features sent relief through the rest of her body.

"I'm so glad you were there, Peter," she said.

"Michael," Peter turned and addressed her brother. "Please get Wendy something to drink. Her mouth has probably gone dry from shock."

Michael obeyed immediately, coming back a moment later from the kitchen with a glass of water.

"I need to head home," Peter said. "But make sure she gets plenty of rest. She'll heal quicker that way." Both brothers nodded their heads vigorously.

"Thank you for saving our sister," John said with feeling.

"Truly, Peter," Wendy said from the couch. "What heroism you showed."

Peter waved his hand to the side. "It was nothing. I'm glad I was there to save you." And with that, Peter bid them goodnight and left, closing the door behind him.

Right after the door shut, John locked it with a hard turn of his wrist, as though the emphasis would keep vermin away indefinitely.

He then turned to Wendy while he rubbed his face with his hand. "Why didn't you call one of us to help with the sn–, I mean the thing?"

"I left my phone at home," Wendy explained.

"Well, you could've shouted for me to come help or gone down to Emily's to get Michael."

Michael nodded, agreeing with John. "I would've come immediately."

"I wasn't thinking straight, or at all," she defended. "Even if I had been, I don't know if I would have wanted to bother you."

"Bother us? Wendy, you're our sister—we would do anything for you," John declared.

The sentiment warmed her heart. Just like Peter being there. Maybe he did care about her. "I'm so grateful Peter was there." Exhaustion flooded her body. "Could you boys help me to my room? I just want to sleep."

Michael assisted her off the couch and down the hall before bringing her some Ibuprofen, a glass of water, and some chocolate.

"Mother always said chocolate helps you feel better," Michael offered.

Wendy took the medicine and chased it down with a piece of chocolate. "She was right."

Her brothers fussed over her for a while longer before she shooed them away and told them she needed to rest. They eventually bid her goodnight and closed her door.

Wendy lay breathing slowly, processing the evening. She decided evening walks were no longer a priority, even if the weather was perfectly lovely. It wasn't worth the risk of coming across a snake again.

～

Peter smiled mischievously to himself as he checked on the gopher snake in a zipped canvas bag in his trunk. It hadn't been that hard to catch in the woods near work. Gopher snakes appeared and behaved so similar to rattlesnakes they were often mistaken for them. But ultimately, it was truly harmless. Wendy didn't need to know that though.

He dropped it off near the mountains to set it free before heading home.

That's not how I anticipated things would go, he thought as he rubbed his stinging arm. He'd given himself a couple scrapes to make it appear as though he'd struggled with the snake. A bandage and some ointment should take care of that.

But it went better than planned.

It was clear that Wendy thought of him as her hero once again, and all was well in Peter's world.

CHAPTER TWELVE

Wendy's emotions told her to go back to class that week to see Evan. Her thoughts cautioned her not to hope for an unrealistic relationship.

The week flew by with an active schedule at the clinic, and suddenly it was Friday. She was simultaneously afraid and excited to see Evan again.

But why should I be excited to see Evan? Peter proved he's still a hero.

She'd reflected on Evan's story throughout the week—how he stowed away on Peter's ship and left Neverland to seek a better future. Her chest constricted with jealousy when she thought about his dating life, but she'd been the one to ask. She didn't know why.

She then rolled her eyes as she admitted to herself that she liked him. But what woman wouldn't? With his height, physique, and those startling blue eyes, it would be impossible not to like him. And he wasn't her enemy anymore. She couldn't deny how she felt around him, and the pull to see him compelled her to return to class.

Karmen picked her up, raising her eyebrows as Wendy sat in the passenger seat.

"What?" Wendy asked while buckling.

"You look like you're gonna vomit, amiga."

"I do not," Wendy retorted.

"Your face is pale and your mouth is all scrunched."

Wendy pulled the visor down and checked her face in the mirror. Karmen was right. Wendy rubbed her face to pull some color back to her cheeks and moved her mouth side to side to erase the frown. Once satisfied with the transformation, she set the visor in place and leaned back in her seat.

"You scared to see someone?" Karmen drove down the road.

"Scared is too strong of a word."

"Nervous but also excited but also freaking out a little," Karmen supplied.

"Anxious," Wendy explained. "But yes, also the words you said."

Karmen parked the car before turning to face Wendy. "I don't know what happened with you two last week—you've been so hush about it." She gave Wendy a pointed look. "But it's okay. If you like each other, just see where things go."

Wendy took a deep breath and let it out before nodding to Karmen and going into the studio.

Class that day focused on blocking. She and Karmen were paired as sparring partners, to Wendy's relief and disappointment. Practicing with Evan during the first class had left her breathless physically and emotionally, but she knew it was better for her to be partnered with Karmen. It was less distracting. And since the clinic had been especially busy that week and they hadn't had time to catch up, she interspersed her story of the snake while they practiced.

"A freaking rattlesnake?" Karmen exclaimed. She lunged and Wendy blocked.

"I thought they stayed in the woods or mountains, but somehow one found its way to my front porch. If Peter hadn't been there when I passed out—"

Karmen paused their match and lifted her mask, her face full of disbelief. "Peter the Player? The one who can't make up his mind and throws rubber snakes at you and can't keep his eyes off other women around you? *That* Peter?"

Wendy huffed and tapped Karmen's foil with her own. "Yes, *that* Peter. Keep going, because I'm not letting you win."

"I'm gonna lose either way, chica. Your skills are on point." Karmen resumed her position and the conversation. "What was Peter doing at your house? I thought he never goes over there."

"He doesn't, but he said he had a feeling he needed to be there that night. Isn't that noble? I'm so glad he was. He caught me just as I passed out. I probably would've hit my head on the sidewalk, got a concussion, and been bitten by the rattlesnake. Then I'd be dead, John would have to take care of Michael—"

"And you wouldn't be too distracted to notice that class is over," came Evan's voice from behind her.

Wendy slipped up her next move and Karmen won their match.

"¡Victoriosa!" Karmen cheered while removing her mask. "It was a fake victory, but still."

Wendy rounded on Evan. "I lost the match because of you."

He stepped close to her, his head tilted down to keep eye contact. "How so?"

The deepness of his forget-me-not blue eyes drew her in and suddenly Wendy forgot what was so important she had to defend herself

on. Her eyes traveled down to his lips, and her mind wandered further
. . .

"She lost because you totally interrupted our girl talk," Karmen answered, pulling Wendy from her fantasy.

Evan smirked as though he could see inside Wendy's mind. "Then it appears she needs a bit of help learning to stay focused while blocking an attack."

"Si, Wendy needs more practice after class," Karmen supplied. Wendy's eyes darted to Karmen's with a plea. *Don't leave me again!*

Karmen's grin implied she knew exactly what Wendy's eyes conveyed, but she didn't care. "I'll pick her up later. Here, teach Wendy how to fight properly." Karmen gave Evan her foil and deserted Wendy as the rest of the class filed out. Oh, she'd have a word or two with Karmen later.

As the last student left the building, Evan tapped Wendy's foil to begin their match and Wendy went into position. She blocked each jab and strike—she'd done this hundreds of times before. This was silly. "I know what I'm doing. I don't need more practice; you just startled me."

Evan raised an eyebrow. "I *know* you know what you're doing. But isn't it good to be crossing swords with each other again?"

"Ha. It certainly is, especially since you aren't trying to kill me."

"I never tried to kill you, Wendy." He advanced on her and her footing took her backward.

"Yes, you did. I know we provoked you to no end, but the vigor with which you and your crew pursued us and the exertion of battle after battle. What other conclusion is there than that you wanted us all dead?" She gained a few steps forward before Evan had her retreating backward again.

"We didn't want you all dead. Well, we wouldn't have minded if Peter had died at some point. But the goal was to wear you all out so you'd leave us alone. You have no idea what it's like to be provoked by Peter's inane antics time and again."

Wendy huffed a laugh. "I do, actually. He hasn't changed much since coming here."

Evan's advance intensified. "You're together, then? You and Peter. I wondered what would become of the two of you."

Wendy scowled while matching Evan's sparring intensity. "How dare you assume such a thing."

"You were always by his side in Neverland. How could anyone assume otherwise?"

Wendy wanted to scream at him. "Tinkerbell was always with him. She made it impossible to gain his full attention. I never truly had a chance with him."

Evan continued to compel Wendy's backward retreat, blow after blow. "And what about now? He's here, she's not. Have you gained your desires with him?"

He'd backed her into the wall. He pressed his foil against hers as she leaned against the wall, both of them catching their breath as they locked eyes with each other.

"Now?" Wendy asked in answer to Evan's questions. Peter had saved her from the snake, but she realized his nearness that day did nothing to her emotionally or physically. Not the way Evan's nearness affected her now.

Evan's chest rose and fell as his breathing evened again. His eyes bore into hers. "What are your desires now, Wendy?" he whispered.

Her eyes automatically fell to Evan's lips.

≈

This tension with Wendy was so thick, Evan could've sliced it with his hook.

But he was no longer Hook. He was Evan, standing in front of Wendy, feeding off the desire in her expression. Her lips parted and her eyes darted between his mouth and eyes.

He knew exactly what she desired, and he intended to give it to her. He took both their foils and dropped them. Then he cupped her face with his hand and watched her eyelids close as her head tilted backward ever so slightly. He leaned in, nuzzling her neck with his nose, his heart hammering as she let out a soft moan of pleasure and moved her hands to his waist. He kissed the corner of her jaw, and she gasped, pulling him closer to her. He moved his mouth up to the corner of her lips, and she fisted his shirt at his hips.

He paused, needing to hear her answer. "What is it you desire, Wendy?" he whispered in the stillness of the room.

Her eyes opened and she met his gaze.

"You," she whispered.

She moved her hands behind his head and pulled his lips to hers. Fire shot through his entire body. He knew Wendy could be passionate when speaking, but he never thought she had this kind of physical passion to her. He absorbed it, moved with it, and swam in it. Her intensity could burn the building to ashes, and he'd willingly go down with the inferno.

Let it burn. Let it burn him till he became nothing and could emerge from the ashes as a truly new man if it meant she wanted him.

CHAPTER THIRTEEN

"W hat kind of workout did you two do?" Karmen asked when she picked Wendy up over an hour later. "You look *disheveled*."

Wendy turned and caught Karmen's smirk and hidden meaning. "We were everything proper," she countered.

Karmen nodded. "Right. So that's why your hair is a hot mess, and your lips are swollen. That's totally proper after fencing with someone for over an hour."

Wendy's head fell forward into her hands. "What am I going to do, Karmen?" she moaned.

"We can always go back, and you can kiss him some more."

Wendy's head snapped back up. "No, I mean, he isn't simply some sexy man I've hooked up with." *Hooked up with*. She found the pun in her sentence and laughed.

"You're scaring me, chica," Karmen said, eyeing Wendy. "And I don't think you mean that the way other people do."

Wendy sobered and continued her thoughts. "He's a man from my past, and it's complicated. John and Michael might not believe he's changed, and then where will we be?"

"So, you need your brothers' approval to date Evan? This is the twenty-first century, not nineteen-fifty. You can date who you want and not care what other people think about it, you know."

"Yes, but they're my brothers." Wendy pictured the hurt on their faces if they thought Hook was still an enemy. Would it come down to choosing them over him? She'd choose her brothers in a heartbeat, but she also wanted to see where this road with Evan led.

Karmen nodded. "I know the three of you are tight. But it's okay to have a relationship for yourself. You won't be with your brothers forever. They're gonna grow up, meet someone, and all that. You know what I mean?"

Wendy bit her lower lip. "I can tell they're already keeping things to themselves. John disappears for a couple hours a few nights a week, saying he's 'going somewhere'. He won't tell us where that is, though. Not even Michael, and they usually tell each other everything. And Michael keeps going over to Emily's to 'work on math', but how many math assignments can they have in one week?"

Karmen pulled up to the townhouse and Wendy searched the street for her brothers' cars. "Case in point, they're not even home right now."

"I mean," Karmen said, "it *is* Friday night. Maybe they got together with friends?"

Wendy sighed. "That's true. Aren't you coming in so I can beat you at a game?" Karmen usually had the car turned off by this point of their Friday girls' nights together.

"Oh, uh," Karmen hedged. "I made plans to see another friend tonight. Our schedules are flip-flopped and it's one of the only times we can catch up."

76

Wendy's heart dropped a little. "Oh, okay." She unbuckled and hugged Karmen. "I hope you enjoy catching up with...him, her?" She waited for Karmen to expound.

But Karmen was sending a text. "Yeah, it'll be fun," she answered distractedly.

Taking that as her cue to go, Wendy bid Karmen a good night and went inside her brotherless townhome. Karmen's car rolled down the street to her next social excursion.

Wendy pulled out a game of solitaire, but the kings in her deck of cards with their dark hair reminded her of Evan. She streamed a period drama, but the accents reminded her of Evan. She listened to music, but the love songs she delighted in only brought more thoughts of Evan to Wendy's mind.

She couldn't escape this. She didn't want to escape this. So she texted him.

Wendy: *How are you still on my mind after I've left you?*

A moment later he responded.

Evan: *Which part of me is on your mind?*

Wendy: *All of you*, she texted while smiling.

Evan: *Are you busy with Karmen?*

Wendy: *No, she said she's meeting up with someone.*

Evan: ... ...

Wendy waited while Evan figured out his words.

Evan: *Can I come over? I know you said you didn't want me to know where you live.*

She texted him the address, and he was at the door within ten minutes.

She opened the door and felt goosebumps over her arms seeing him in her doorway, appearing unsure of himself as he ran his left arm across the back of his neck. She widened the door, and he entered, taking in the front room of her home.

"You live here with your brothers?" he asked.

"Yes, but they're both gone right now."

His eyes came back to her. "You're alone?"

Wendy nodded, and Evan's face became comically quizzical.

"What is it?" she asked.

"Can you be trusted alone with me, Wendy?" he teased.

"Me? It was you who started—"

She was interrupted by Evan's mouth on hers. She pulled him to her, and they went on for some minutes before pulling away.

Evan stroked her hair back with his left hand while his right arm encircled her torso. "I need to leave." Wendy's eyebrows contracted in question, and he answered. "I could kiss you all night, but I know there are limits. Let's do this properly."

Her eyes searched his. "When can we see each other again?"

"Work has me in every direction this week. It might not be till next Friday."

"After class?"

He nodded. "But I'll show you a fun evening."

"As in, a real date?" Her heart leaped at the idea.

He chuckled. "Yes, a real date. You sound as though you haven't been on one in a while."

"I haven't. Unless you count the monthly meetings with Peter. But that can't be counted as dating. Not if he insists on ignoring me while I'm right there."

Evan's face hardened. "Peter has always been an idiot, but behaving as you describe it makes him the king of all idiocy." He took some deep breaths, and the anger left his face. Then he brought his hand up and cupped her chin. "You should never be treated that way. You are astonishing, Wendy. Your mind, your spirit, the care you give, the work you put into life. It's remarkable."

Her eyes darted between his as her heart pulsed in her throat. "How long have you felt that way?"

"How does one count time in Neverland?"

Wendy shook her head. "One doesn't count time there."

"Then I can't say exactly, but it's been a long time."

Wendy's heart leaped.

He kissed her, and though she ached for him to stay, she knew it was best for him to leave. He brushed his thumb over her lips, kissed her forehead gently, and bid her goodnight.

CHAPTER FOURTEEN

The next day dawned dreary and overcast, and by the time Peter got to work, the rain was coming down heavily. Heavy rain meant slower business as client after client called to cancel their excursions.

There were too many guides than was necessary for the workload. Tessa, ever helpful, offered to stay in case a group came in for a trek, so everyone else went home. Then it was just Peter and Tessa at the Trek cabin. What a lark he'd had with her the previous weekend.

He'd gotten more than he'd anticipated that night. He hadn't had that much fun for at least a few months. Nothing immoral or scandalous—that wasn't Peter's style. Nor was it Tessa's, being the straight arrow that she was. Simply making out was enjoyable in its own right.

Peter slipped into the back room where he knew Tessa would be organizing supplies. He looked both ways but didn't see her. Then slender hands turned his shoulders around and pulled him behind the door. Those same slender hands fisted his shirt.

Ah, there she is, Peter thought satisfactorily.

Tessa stood on her toes and kissed Peter fiercely. He kissed her back and wound his arms around her waist. They carried on for several minutes in each other's arms, neither one in a hurry to stop.

I'm winning this game. The rule-following straight arrow is bending, after all. Peter inwardly smiled with pride.

Tessa finally pulled back from Peter. "Hey," she said, out of breath. "I've missed you all week."

"I know." He winked at her and kissed her again.

Tessa chuckled. "You taste like mint," she said while her hands tentatively explored his hair. He knew this type of intimate expression was still new territory for her.

He flashed her a smile. "I've been chewing gum all afternoon," he said. "I hoped that after work we would pick up where we left off last week, but you started sooner than I anticipated."

She smiled and pulled him closer. She really was a good kisser. He wouldn't keep pursuing this game if she wasn't.

Peter lifted his head from Tessa's and gave her his most charming, roguish smile. He could tell it took her breath away.

"We should go out front in case a client comes in and sees us," Peter told her, furrowing his brows. "That would be embarrassing for you."

Tessa's eyebrows drew in. "For me? What do you mean?" she asked innocently.

"I'm the rule-bender, you're the rule-follower. Wouldn't you be mortified if you were seen with me?"

Tessa looked at him disbelievingly. "No, I like being with you."

"You're just saying that." He turned his eyes to the floor, feigning modesty.

"No, really," she countered. "I think people are judging you too much. You're a good guy, and . . ."

His head came up, curious what she would say. "And?"

She shrugged. "I really like you. I know I like to stick to my rules and all that, but maybe I've been too strict. You've helped me relax a little, and I've felt so good this past week after being with you last weekend. No guy I've dated has done that for me."

He gave her his knock-out grin. "Happy to help."

He leaned in to kiss her again, but she put her finger to his mouth. "But you're right. It's time to close the cabin. Then we can hang out more."

Peter sighed. She still had that responsibility-thing in her. No matter. He'd do as she suggested to win this pleasurable game.

<hr />

After Outdoor Adventure Trek was closed and locked up, Peter and Tessa went to her place to "hang out." This was where they'd hung out (in the literal sense of the phrase) last weekend when she invited him to be with her and her roommates.

Peter's thoughts drifted to that night a week ago. He'd felt the vibe that Tessa wasn't merely being her usual sweet-self by inviting him over—she was genuinely attracted to him. He worked with that all evening, subtly flirting and giving her most of his attention. She'd begun finding ways to touch him—a swat on his arm, a nudge with her shoulder. He slipped his hand into hers at one point, and though she tensed at first, she didn't pull away. After that, he'd suggested a walk, just the two of them. In the moonlight beneath a flowering tree, he made the first move by kissing her. He'd gone for a gentle kiss to test her out, but she'd responded by kissing him with intensity and kissing him *a lot*. Who knew this innocent girl had so much desire hiding beneath her facade?

And all this even though he knew she had a boyfriend.

"My boyfriend would be so mad at me if he knew I was with you right now," Tessa had said with wide eyes, her hand over her mouth.

"You have a boyfriend?" Peter had asked, pretending ignorance with wide eyes.

"I thought you knew."

"I'm so sorry. I should go home," Peter had said, shaking his head.

"Stay," Tessa had pleaded while grasping his arm. "Don't go. I've never been with someone like you. I feel free to be myself, free to relax into life."

"Well," Peter had hesitated. "If you're sure…"

Tessa pursed her lips and nodded.

"Tessa?" Peter had murmured against her lips.

"Mmm?" she'd murmured back.

"You're sure he won't find out?" He really didn't want to be retaliated against by a jealous boyfriend.

"I can keep a secret," she'd promised.

His thoughts returned to the present, though the location and activity were the same as they'd been a week ago. Her roommates were out doing other things, so Peter and Tessa were alone in her apartment. Something she wouldn't have allowed a week ago.

Making out with Tessa sent pleasure all through Peter's body. But since he'd reached his goal of bending this rule-following goodie-girl, he decided his game was finished and it was time to move on.

But he was totally unprepared to hear that Tessa had broken up with her boyfriend.

"You what?" he exclaimed when she told him.

"Peter," she said with shocked eyes after his reaction. "I thought you'd be excited. Now you and I can be together without secrets."

"But what happened with your boyfriend?" Peter's mind went reeling. Now Tessa expected to be official with him? What if her boyfriend came after him?

Her shoulders fell while she exhaled. "He and I had this big argument. I told him he was too straight-laced, and he needed to relax, and he told me I'd changed too much. I figured since he was being judgmental, and you and I have been together anyway ...Well, I just broke up with him." She looked expectantly at Peter, who felt his irritation written all over his features.

"Peter." She rubbed his arms. "This is good, right? I thought you'd be excited."

"Tessa, we're not exclusive," he explained, gesturing between them and shaking his head.

She swallowed and dropped her hands to her side. "What do you mean?"

"I just wanted to see how far you would bend." He shrugged.

Tessa's eyebrows came down. "What?"

Peter laughed at her ignorance. "You're so uptight about things. I thought it'd be fun to see you let loose, so I made it my goal. And it worked."

"Let loose ... Are you playing with me?" Tessa exhaled disbelievingly. "That's ridiculous."

Not my fault she's been so narrow in her standards. Where's the fun in that? I helped her see the enjoyable side of life. She said so herself, he justified.

Tessa's eyes welled with tears. Her hand flew out faster than his reflexes could respond, and she slapped him soundly across the face.

"How dare you?" Her voice had never sounded so low and dangerous. "How dare you play with me—with my feelings and my hopes. I thought you cared about me, but it was just for some twisted goal? You should be so *ashamed*, Peter." She hissed the last sentence in a way that made Peter feel a smidgen of guilt.

He pushed the guilt down where it belonged and rubbed the place she'd slapped him. "How dare *I*? What about *you*?" He gestured toward her. "You broke up with your boyfriend, not even knowing what I would have to say on the matter. If you want to belong to someone so badly, go back to him. I can't believe you just hit me." He rubbed the spot again. "And you said yourself I made you feel free and wonderful. I have that effect on women. You should feel honored that I chose to help you."

A tear rolled down Tessa's face. "You have a problem, Peter. You can't mess with people like this. Where's your honor, your empathy? People have emotions, but you don't care."

Peter rolled his eyes, and she gestured to his face. "Like that. You're rolling your eyes while being corrected. You think other people need to change instead of you."

He folded his arms and glared at her. Was she finished with her silly tirade yet? Apparently not.

"Have you ever heard of narcissism?" Tessa asked.

Peter scoffed. "That's a bit dramatic."

"One symptom of a narcissist is denial. Another is projection. You've just shown both."

"How would you know about any of that?"

Tessa paused. "I grew up with narcissistic parents. It's a miracle they stayed together as long as they did. Our home was filled with entitlement, self-centeredness, justification, and rule-bending." She shook her head. "I should've seen the signs in your behavior, but you intrigued me, and I just wanted a chance with you. Instead, you messed with me."

"And *you* slapped me." How could she not see the fault in her own actions?

She pointed to the door. "Get out," she said evenly. "You are the most self-centered, immature, inconsiderate, selfish ..."

"I get it," Peter interrupted. "You're upset with me." Who was *she* to throw rude words at him?

She shook her head. "Just get out, Peter. Good luck with your life if you won't change." She waited until he moved toward the door. The second he was outside, she shut and locked it.

Girls, he thought. *So dramatic and judgmental. Narcissistic? Ridiculous. I've grown to be quite the heartbreaker. Well, I won the game. Ha—the cleverness of me!*

He smiled to himself and went home, ignoring the niggle of guilt from Tessa's words.

CHAPTER FIFTEEN

Wendy wondered how being with Evan could feel so *normal*.

He bowled a strike and lifted his fist as Wendy clapped. His smile was Hook's, yet it wasn't. There was still that same roguish element that had her pulse pounding in Neverland, but now it was paired with a wholesomeness that gave Wendy reassurance that her heart was safe with him. And oh, how lovely that was.

Karmen's perpetual smile during class that day had Wendy rolling her eyes as they practiced footwork. And when Karmen dropped Wendy off at home after class and said, "Behave tonight," Wendy verbally jabbed her friend right back with a smirk and said, "Same to you and your mystery man."

"How do you know I'm meeting up with a man?" Karmen said while a corner of her mouth rose.

"Your smile only confirms my suspicions. And you'd only ditch me for a man." Karmen had given her a doubtful glance. "You know I'm right," Wendy smirked.

Karmen sighed. "You are muy inteligente, amiga."

Wendy's mind came back to the present and her bowling date with Evan. Which she was sorely losing at.

After her fourth gutter ball, she suggested, "Should we just go get ice cream now?"

"You've never been a quitter, Wendy Darling," Evan countered. "There's only two sets left. Maybe fortune will favor you."

Well, fortune favored Evan with two more strikes, which left Wendy with no luck and two more gutter balls.

"You are really bad at this," Evan joked while taking her hand after the game.

"But I didn't quit," she pointed out.

"That you did not." Evan tugged her toward him and kissed her forehead. "Be proud of yourself for persisting in a losing battle."

"Does this mean it's time for ice cream?"

He took her to an ice cream parlor, where they downed double scoops in waffle cones.

"We never had flavors like these in my childhood," Wendy said as she took another bite of her salted caramel and chocolate chip ice cream. "How can you eat plain vanilla?"

Evan swallowed his bite. "Neverland doesn't have ice cream. And vanilla is the most expensive spice in the world. This is a delicacy."

"You could've at least added a topping. Here." She scooped some chocolate chips from hers and set them on top of Evan's.

He stared at her. "Shouldn't that be considered unsanitary?"

She leaned forward. "Every time you kiss me, we share those same germs." She nodded to the chocolate chips.

He kept eye contact while bringing the ice cream to his mouth and took a big bite of the chocolate chips. Wendy snickered and took another bite of hers.

Normal. As though they'd both been raised during this time period. Perhaps if they had been, they'd have met at a social gathering somewhere. They'd exchange numbers and be like the myriad of couples around them.

And she wouldn't have to keep their involvement a secret from her brothers. But her brothers had secrets of their own. John continued to be elsewhere without explanation several nights each week, and Michael still had daily math assignments with Emily. Wendy hadn't pressed them for more information, trusting they had their own reasons for keeping things to themselves.

Just as Wendy had her own reasons for keeping her relationship with Evan to herself. Evan, however, disagreed with those reasons.

"You can drop me off across the street," Wendy told him at the end of their date as they neared her home.

He shook his head. "I wish you'd just tell them."

"But what if they don't trust you? What if they don't believe you've changed, and they don't support my being with you?"

He glanced at her. "Do *you* trust me and believe I've changed?"

"I wouldn't let you kiss me if I didn't."

He smiled at that before turning serious. "Do they trust you to make your own decisions?"

Wendy hadn't considered that. Her brothers had always shown complete trust in her, and she'd never given them a reason to doubt her.

"Do you think they'll trust you in the future if you keep this a secret now?" Evan asked.

Wendy sighed. "But what if I tell them and they get angry and ..." She pondered the worst that could happen. Her brothers would be angry and her credibility with them would diminish. It would hurt her emotionally and rift them relationally. She voiced her thoughts to Evan.

He nodded. "I understand the three of you have a unique bond. It would be painful to see that disrupted." He parked his Jeep across the street from her townhome, then turned to her. "But the longer you keep us a secret," he took her hand and kissed the top of it, "the more hurt they will be when they find out."

Wendy leaned her head against her seat. "I know you're right. The secrets the three of us are keeping from each other has already shifted the feeling in our home." She closed her eyes and exhaled. "But maybe I could tell them another day?"

She opened one eye and peeked at Evan, who frowned. "Are you ashamed of me?"

"What? No!" She sat up and laced her fingers through his. "It's just, I want their support. Being with you is important to me."

Evan leaned in, kissing Wendy in a way that made her forget her worries. She wanted this relationship with him. It was just so right. They'd been given a chance to be together, and she didn't want to mess it up by her brothers' judgments coming between them.

Evan rested his forehead against hers. "I trust you," he whispered.

"Thank you," she whispered in response.

"I'll see you at class next week." He stroked her face and kissed her forehead before she left the car, crossed the street, and entered her townhouse. She decided that for now, she'd appreciate each moment she had with Evan and think about how to tell her brothers later.

Chapter Sixteen

The next week, Evan was on cloud nine every time he thought about his date with Wendy. Or even just every time he thought of her. A few times Coby had to snap Evan out of his thoughts to return to the present task.

Coby elbowed Evan from the driver's seat. "You're distracted, dude. But, like, in a good way. You're smiling a lot today."

Evan's smile grew as he glanced at Coby from the passenger seat of the moving van. "I can't deny it." His thoughts truly were just a jumble of Wendy.

"You gonna give me details, or will you make me guess every option under the sun?"

"That friend I reconnected with at class? I took her out last week-end."

"And?" Coby prodded.

"And what?"

"Things must be pretty good with her if you're smiling so much."

Evan's torso warmed as he thought of his kisses with Wendy. "They are."

"Awesome," Coby said. "Where do you know her from?"

"You wouldn't believe me if I told you." He laughed humorlessly, shaking his head.

What would Coby do if I actually said, "I met her in Neverland"? The thought was ludicrous.

"Well, then, what's her name?" Coby asked, elbowing Evan again.

"Wendy." Saying her name aloud filled Evan's senses with serenity.

"Hey," Coby exclaimed, turning to face Evan. "I know a girl named Wendy."

"Whoa! Eyes on the road, Coby." Evan pointed to the street ahead as they nearly collided with an oncoming car. Coby turned back to the steering wheel, his shoulders hunched.

"Sorry, man." Then he brightened again. "I didn't know there were so many Wendys out there."

Evan worked to calm his pulse from the almost-accident. "Where do you know your friend Wendy from?"

"She's the girl I wanted to set you up with, the girl with the two brothers I went camping with," Coby explained.

"Did you all grow up together?" Evan asked, his curiosity overriding his stress.

"I guess you could say that." Coby tilted his head from side to side. "Seems like we were kids forever until we all came out here."

"Where did you all come from?"

Coby flicked his eyes to Evan, smiling. "You wouldn't believe me if I told you." His voice was a passable imitation of Evan's accent.

Evan tossed his head back and laughed. "Keep working on the accent." He peered at the street ahead. "You don't think I'd believe you?"

"Nuh-uh."

"Tell me, and we'll see," Evan challenged while smirking. He didn't know much about twenty-first century locations, but Coby couldn't have come from somewhere outrageous.

Coby took in a slow breath and exhaled quickly. "We all came from Neverland," he said in a rush, grimacing.

Evan's smile dropped. How would Coby know to joke about Neverland? Maybe a random coincidence?

"I told you you wouldn't believe me," Coby said self-consciously.

Evan's mouth opened and closed several times to form a response. "I'd love to believe you," he said. "It's just . . . it's improbable." He'd been reunited with Wendy, but what was the likelihood he'd find another Neverland runaway?

Coby pursed his lips before answering. "You wouldn't believe what's actually possible, Evan. Okay, I told you where I came from. Now it's your turn. After my answer, I'm sure I'd believe anything you say."

How could he respond? *I came from Neverland. But you weren't there, Coby.*

Or had he been?

Peter and the rest had dispersed after the ship crash landed in the USA. Evan had no idea what Peter or the Lost Boys were up to now. Was Coby a former Lost Boy? Evan would've recognized him, right?

But Coby had said it felt as though he and his friends had been kids forever. Like a Lost Boy. And after they'd had time in the real world to grow up, they might not be immediately recognizable.

Evan peered closely at Coby. Strong build, curly hair...

Curly hair?

What on earth? It can't be . . .

He studied Coby's facial features. "Curly?" Evan voiced with disbelief. Yes, he could see the former Lost Boy now, in context. But how was it possible?

Coby stiffened at the name. He glanced quickly at Evan with shrewd eyes. "Why'd you call me that? No one calls me that now."

"I think we'd better finish the day's work, then let's talk." Evan ran his hand through his hair. So much to process. He'd unknowingly worked with one of the Lost Boys for at least a year. But that meant Coby—Curly—had been unknowingly working with the former Captain Hook for at least a year. How would he react when he found out who Evan really was?

The day passed without much spoken between them. Evan's mind tried to formulate an explanation of who he was and who he wasn't. When at last they returned their van and supplies at the end of the day, Evan suggested they go for a drive and talk. They drove nowhere in particular while Evan brought up the topic.

"You were known as Curly in Neverland, correct?"

Coby eyed Evan warily from the passenger seat. "Yeah. But how do you know that? Did one of the guys tell you? I'm not insane, I promise. I really did come from there."

Evan shook his head. "The status of your sanity is intact with me. I believe you because . . ." Was there any way to cushion this blow? He plowed forward. "You knew me there as Captain Hook."

Coby flinched and scrutinized Evan, who paused while waiting to turn right at a traffic light. When Coby's probing eyes met Evan's, recognition hit. "It's that color. I don't know why I didn't connect it before now. I've never seen anyone with that eye color but you. Holy crap." He unbuckled his seatbelt and tried to open the door, but the light turned green, and Evan had already begun to move the car forward.

"What are you doing?" he cried as Coby fumbled with the door.

"You tried to kill us!" Coby shot back.

"I've worked with you for over a year. Have I ever tried to kill you in Reality?"

Coby paused and Evan pulled the car over. "You're not going to kill me now, are you?" Coby asked as he glanced over his shoulder.

Evan's shoulders slumped. "If I was going to kill you, or any of the others, I would've done so by now." He told of his following them as a stowaway, and of the effort he'd made to morph his life to the opposite of what it'd been before. No more villainy.

"Oh," Coby responded with a perplexed expression. "So, you're not going to kill me?"

"No," Evan chuckled. "I'd be out of an excellent co-worker if I did."

Coby gave a humble smile and relaxed into his seat. "Well, you're doing a good job of changing. I didn't even recognize you. And now you're even dating someone. Wait." His face lit up. "You said you're dating a girl named Wendy. Are you dating *Wendy*-Wendy?"

Evan's pulse sped up thinking of her and he nodded.

Coby made an explosion sound and extended his fingers above his head. "Mind. Blown. Her brothers know, right? And Peter and the other guys?"

"No, not even her brothers know." Much to his chagrin.

"Why? She's always been tight with them. Wouldn't she want them to know you the way you are now? Because you're nothing like the you from before. They've gotta see that."

"She's afraid they won't support our relationship."

"No," Coby said, waving a hand. "They'd be cool about it. John and Michael love Wendy. She's always there for them. You guys should tell them."

Evan nodded. He knew that each day their secret was kept from John and Michael would make their support more difficult to receive.

Coby buckled up again, ready for their drive to continue. "You guys go tell them. What's the worst that could happen?"

CHAPTER SEVENTEEN

Wendy looked forward to Friday all week. Karmen wouldn't stop teasing her about it. Wendy, in turn, teased Karmen about her mystery man.

"Is he tall, dark, and handsome?" Wendy asked during a brief break at the clinic.

Karmen's smile spread. "Si, and he is so charming and inteligente. I'm going to see him tonight again." She squealed, earning a reproving look from one of the pediatricians. She lowered her voice. "I'll pick you up tonight for class."

"I'll drive myself over," Wendy countered. "That way you can meet with your mystery man sooner."

After work, Wendy changed into her gym clothes and went searching for her sneakers. She'd just spotted them under her bed when there was a knock at the door.

Who on earth could that be? she wondered.

Her heart leaped. *Maybe it's Evan. He's come to escort me to class, or something like that.*

Elated by the idea, she grabbed her shoes and trotted to the door, her lips stretching in a smile. Her smile faltered when she opened the door and saw Peter standing on her doorstep.

He lifted an eyebrow in irritation at Wendy's unenthusiastic greeting. "Well, don't look so excited to see me."

"Sorry. I just wasn't expecting to see you here. Come in." Wendy opened the door wider, and he entered, standing expectantly in the doorway.

"You should go get ready."

"I am ready," she said, gesturing to her activewear. "I'm headed to fencing class right now."

Peter scrunched his face. "Oh, the fencing class. I completely forgot about that." He chuckled. "I guess I'm not doing that. No hard feelings?" He offered her his fist.

She fist-bumped him, relieved he'd never gone to the class. What a mess that would've been. "No hard feelings, Peter. I figured you'd just forgotten. Don't worry about it."

"I won't," he smiled charmingly at her and stepped forward. "But tonight, you're not going *fencing*. You'll be doing something better." He waggled his eyebrows and smirked.

Panic seized Wendy's chest. What was Peter talking about? Had she forgotten some commitment she'd made? What about Evan?

"What are you talking about, Peter?" she asked, chuckling nervously. She glanced outside the open door. She needed to leave soon or she'd be late.

Peter pulled his phone out of his pocket with a flourish and waved it tantalizingly from side to side.

"New phone?" Wendy asked in confusion.

"No, there's tickets on my screen, see? I'm taking you out on a date, Wendy."

Wendy stared at him in disbelief. "Oh," was all she could manage to say. Peter's thoughtfulness surprised her.

She was also mildly irked he was just *now* springing this on her.

"That was kind of you, Peter," she said. "A date with you is a kind gesture, but I have a prior commitment tonight. It would be better for you to ask me in advance next time."

"A kind gesture?" Peter scowled for a heartbeat then smoothed his features. "Well, I vote you come with me tonight. You can skip one class, you know. It can't be that big of a deal to miss."

"Peter," she said placatingly. "I didn't ask for your vote. It was sweet of you to invite me, but I'm not available tonight." She looked at him with lifted eyebrows. "And I need to leave now or I'll be late."

"Wendy," Peter whined. "Why won't you just come with me?" He sagged his shoulders and huffed childishly.

Throwing a fit to manipulate me; what rubbish.

Wendy stared at him as a firm parent would with a tantrum-throwing toddler, an expression she'd often used with him during their arguments in Neverland. Peter's face instantly changed from childish-mode to victim-mode.

"Wasn't it sweet of me to think of you and get us tickets for the theater tonight?" he said, sighing.

Nice try, Peter.

He stood with an expectant look, watching Wendy for several seconds. Then he broke the silence and turned defensive. "And I totally already asked you. And you said yes. I think you just forgot." He shook his head and pursed his lips in disapproval.

"I did no such thing." Peter's manipulative tactics wouldn't work on Wendy.

But then his face turned contrite as he looked down and dropped his hand to his side. When he looked up at Wendy, she wanted to believe the innocence she saw on his face.

"*Please*, Wendy," he implored. "I just want to spend time with you. To be with you. Please."

His words loosened her defenses the slightest bit, but she remained unmoved. "No." She'd rather be with Evan, and she hadn't made any commitment to Peter tonight.

He sighed. "Well, alright. At least let me give you a ride to class."

Wendy considered the offer. Evan could take her home afterward, or they could just start their date right after. "Very well."

All traces of sadness left Peter's face, replaced by a half smile.

~

Ha! Peter thought. *I did it—I bested Wendy. Thought she could see past my strategies, did she?*

He rushed her to his car, without any intention of taking her to class. He sped down her street toward the main road.

"Peter—slow down," Wendy cried, clutching the car door with one hand.

"It's fine." He waved away her concern. "I know what I'm doing. Now," he said to change the irksome subject. "Are you curious what these tickets are for?"

"Yes, extremely curious." She exhaled in a huff. "But you're taking me to class, remember?"

"Oh yes, that's right. Where should I go?"

"To the martial arts studio on Main Street," she said, relief in her voice.

He glanced at Wendy with a flash of irritation. "Fine. I'll tell you what I had planned for us tonight on our way there."

Peter spoke of the grand plans he had for them that evening—dinner at an eclectic new restaurant and then going to see *The Phantom of the Opera*. He had Wendy completely distracted all the way to the freeway, heading to the restaurant until it was too late to turn around.

"Peter," she cried out in panic. "You said you'd take me to class, but you forgot to go to Main."

"*I* forgot? I believe it was *you* who failed to give me directions."

"You know where Main Street is," she accused. "Take me to class like you said you would."

What's so special about it, anyway? Nothing that can't take a back seat to an evening with me.

He glanced at her. "Isn't this exciting, though? A spontaneous date with me. I'm sorry about your class, but we have a schedule to maintain if we're to be on time for tonight's plans." He hoped he sounded sincere enough to placate her because he was so sick of hearing about that ridiculous fencing class.

Wendy checked the time on her phone, then began texting. Peter swiped the phone from her hand.

"Peter!" she shouted.

"How can you focus on an evening with me if you're distracted with this?" He pocketed her phone where she couldn't reach it.

"Of all the—Take me back, *now*." Wendy faced him, her expression full of unspoken threats.

102

But Peter was in charge. He'd always been in charge, except when they came to Reality and the Lost Boys stopped following his lead. And now Wendy had it in her mind that some silly class was more important than him. No, he'd take charge once again.

"You can miss one class, Wendy. And we'll have a grand time tonight."

She shifted in her seat, her elbow on the passenger door with her head in her hand. She stared at the passing scenery.

Oh, great. Now she's upset. Peter decided to use some of his other strategies to placate her.

"You look lovely tonight. That shade of blue really brightens your eyes. And are those earrings new?" he asked.

She turned to stare at him stone-faced, unamused, and unmoved by his flattery.

He tried again. "It's a lovely time for a drive. Do you see that tree over there? Pink blossoms everywhere. The same shade as your lips." He turned on his charming smile and glanced at her.

Not only was she still stone-faced, but she'd raised that blasted eyebrow at him. He hated when she did that, like he'd done something wrong.

Why does she have to be so problematic? Fine. I'll cut to the chase and go straight for contrition. Even though I hate doing it.

He paused, then sighed in remorse. He schooled his features to appear repentant, dropping his shoulders in a show of surrender.

"I'm sorry, Wendy," he said in a soft voice. "That was important to you." He shook his head as though berating himself for his mistake. "I wanted to take you on a date so much, but what a mess I've made of things. Can you forgive me for causing you such distress? Are we still friends?" He turned to her with a pleading look and his best puppy dog eyes.

Come on, Wendy. Take the proffered olive branch and get over it, he thought.

Wendy sighed, her stone-face giving way to mere irritation. She huffed, but Peter didn't care.

She took a deep breath and slowly let it out. "It *is* important to me, but I know you're excited about being with me tonight. And yes, we're still friends." She folded her arms and turned to face forward.

Ha! I've bested her again.

"Thank you, Wendy." He was done with that conversation—he could only do contrition for so long. Being in the wrong wasn't his style.

"So, have you ever seen *Phantom*?" he asked, changing the subject.

"No," she sighed. "But from what I understand, the story itself takes place around the time I grew up in London. I've been to the actual Opera House in Paris. Mother and Father took us to France a few years before they died."

"Well," Peter said, "I enjoyed it immensely. I've seen it before." He turned toward Wendy with raised eyebrows.

"Oh?" Wendy blinked. "How long ago?"

"About a year ago," he said, smiling and settling into the driver seat, one hand on the steering wheel with his other elbow leaning out the window. "Some friends insisted they take me to Vegas to see it. What a wonderful time." He chuckled fondly at the memory.

"Las Vegas?" Wendy asked. "Who did you go with?"

"I went with a group of girls, clients who went on a trek last year. I told them I'd never seen *Phantom*, and they set out to rectify that." He chuckled again. "Marvelous weekend, that was."

When Wendy gave no response, he looked over at her. She was scowling again. She folded her arms across her chest and turned toward the passenger side window.

So touchy. Not my fault no one's ever insisted she go to Vegas for a weekend.

The silence in the car persisted all the way to the parking lot of the restaurant. Peter put the car in park, turned off the ignition, and sat back in his seat with a sigh.

Why does Wendy have to make the evening difficult? Time for a dose of that charm she can't resist.

"Wendy, I'm sorry if I said something that upset you," Peter said in a low voice. He reached out and placed a hand on her shoulder. She flinched but turned to him. He gave her an alluring, mischievous smile—one that he rarely used on women (though he did use it), and that almost always had Wendy swooning. Her features shifted from angry to deer-in-the-headlights. Then she shook her head and turned toward her window again.

"You can stop using your tricks on me, Peter," she said in a soft voice. "I know you use those on other girls. I'm nothing special to you." She shook her head. "You could have any girl you want, and you choose to fly through several without any intention of landing on the ground."

She turned to face him, her eyes glossy with tears. "You should've taken me to class, but you didn't. I thought I'd give you the benefit of the doubt, but your insincere methods continue. So let's get this evening over with."

Peter was dumbfounded. When had she become immune to his tactics? *I must've used them on her too many times*, he realized.

Despite her despondent mood, he was still determined to get that Number-One-Hero spot back and to take control of the situation, to regain a sense of normalcy his life had lost since they'd left Neverland.

There was one thing he hadn't tried with Wendy, but he'd need to save that amorous tactic for the right moment. For now, he needed to do damage control. He *hated* damage control—girls could be so high maintenance.

"Get the evening over with? Wendy," he soothed, patting her arm. "This will be a night to remember. Just you and me, Wendy and Peter. Let's put the past behind us and go eat. I bet you're hungry. Maybe that's why you're struggling this evening." He patted her arm again, unbuckled his seatbelt, and made to open his door.

Wendy rounded on him. "My *struggle* this evening," she said heatedly, "has nothing to do with hunger, and everything to do with your selfishness and how insignificant I feel when I'm around you."

Peter stopped and turned toward her. "Insignificant?" he asked, genuinely confused. "What do you mean?"

Wendy tilted her chin down, scowling. "Whenever I'm with you, you can't stay focused on me. You talk about other women. Your eyes wander. And as if that wasn't enough, you go so far as to *flirt* with other women from across the room, or even right in front of me. And *that* is why I feel insignificant with you, Peter."

She turned her body further toward him and curled her hands around the seat. "Do you realize this is the first time you've ever asked me out since we left Neverland?"

"But . . ." He blinked, grasping for justification. "We meet up once each month—just you and me. You know, at the bakery and all that," he finished lamely. Those weren't dates, and he knew it.

And he could tell Wendy knew that he knew it, if her dubious expression was any indication.

Time for a tactic change. "Is there someone else?" He narrowed his eyes.

"What?" She blinked.

Good, she's distracted.

"Are you comparing me with someone else? And I just keep coming up short, don't I?" He shook his head in disapproval. "Bad form, Wendy. Friends don't do that to each other." He folded his arms across his chest.

"Blast it, Peter," she answered with a disbelieving look on her face. "When did *I* become the problem? This has nothing to do with who I'm dating."

Hold on! She's dating someone?

He was livid. He had no control over her dating life. "Did you just say 'who' you're dating? Who *are* you dating?" he raised his voice.

He didn't want to *date* Wendy, but he had to know who the competition for her attention was. As exhausting as this pursuit was becoming, maybe he could do something to win her loyalty back.

"That has nothing to do with this, Peter!" she shouted back. "We aren't talking about who I'm dating, we're talking about how I feel like a nobody when I'm around you."

Wendy stopped and relaxed her shoulders, taking deep breaths while closing her eyes.

Peter followed suit. He might not like what he heard from Wendy, but he didn't want to shout at her.

"But you *are* dating someone?" he asked.

Wendy scowled. "Is this some sort of love triangle for you, Peter?"

"Just answer the question," he said, scowling back.

Her eyes met his straight on. "Yes," she said unashamedly. "I am."

His scowl deepened. "For how long?"

"We've been reacquainted for a few weeks."

"'Reacquainted'? What's that supposed to mean? Surely not one of the Lost Boys." He ran a hand through his hair. "Anyone I know?"

Wendy stayed silent, so he turned to glare at her.

She stared at his eyes. But she didn't answer him directly. "You know a lot of people, Peter." She shrugged, and that was all the answer he got.

"Fine, be that way," he said. "Let's just go eat." He climbed out of the car, slamming the door.

CHAPTER EIGHTEEN

P eter stormed through the parking lot, leaving Wendy in the car, and abandoning all chivalry. Maybe he was too angry to have even thought of opening her door. Wendy sat there for a few minutes before getting out.

This was ridiculous. She didn't want to fight with him—she didn't have the energy anymore. He'd done thoughtless things to her in over-abundance, and arguing with him syphoned her energy every time.

Thankfully, dinner went better than the car ride. Bite by bite, Wendy tried to be polite. She held her tongue when Peter said some-thing thoughtless. She tried not to bristle each time he flirted with the waitress or other women in the restaurant. Peter was Peter—she should have accepted that a long time ago. It was easier to enjoy the evening when she didn't take offense.

Soon it was time to head to the theater. Peter had secured them seats in the balcony, where they could see and hear everything clearly. At least *that* was thoughtful. The musical itself helped her forget her troubled thoughts, with its fullness of emotion, color, hauntingly beautiful music, and a bittersweet ending.

She discovered she'd been crying when the curtains fell at the end of the musical. She searched her bag for tissues and dabbed her eyes.

Peter's eyes widened in shock when he saw her wiping tears away. "It wasn't all that bad." He smacked her on the back.

"Peter, I was crying, not choking," Wendy said, trying to laugh through a cough. "And I wasn't crying because it was bad. It was so emotional that it brought me to tears."

The ride home was uneventful. And late. Wendy didn't realize how long the musical had been. John and Michael would be asleep by now. She hoped they hadn't worried about her.

Peter drove around the corner from her townhouse and found a spot to park.

"There should be adequate parking near my door," she said.

He turned the car off, unbuckled his seatbelt, waggled his eyebrows at Wendy, then got out of the car.

What was that about?

This time he opened her door and helped her out. When she stepped out of the car, he pulled her in tight against him and kissed her possessively.

Wendy was too shocked at first to stop him. She'd fantasized this moment for years, and he was just as good a kisser as she'd imagined. From a distance, she heard shouting and then something crashed down the street.

Her wits caught up with her, and she pushed Peter away as fast as she could.

"Are you daft?" she cried while her fingers touched her lips.

"Oh, come on, Wendy," Peter said, dismissing her concern with a wave of his hand. "Admit it—you've wanted me to do that for a *long* time." He pulled his smolder out and reached to pull her to him again.

She took a step back. "Maybe." Then she shook her head. "But not for the last while. Not any longer." She folded her arms across her chest and took another step back.

Peter scowled. "Since you started dating someone?"

"Since I realized you treat me like a nobody." She scowled back at him. "You think you can muddle with people's emotions, that others don't have feelings? Where's your empathy, Peter? Do you really think others should change just to please you?"

His face registered discomfort for the barest of moments before darkening again. "Fine," he said while straightening. "You had your opportunity just now. You didn't take it. Your loss." He dropped his hands and stomped toward the driver's side of his car. "And you're welcome for the fine evening, by the way," he called over his shoulder.

"Thank you," she responded with sarcasm.

He stopped and cupped his hand around his ear. "Sorry, I didn't hear that," he said belligerently.

"Thank you for the lovely evening," she forced herself to say.

He turned and approached her, his expression smug. "I'll walk you to your door."

"How benevolent of you." After this, she'd cancel their monthly rendezvous. She'd had enough of his company.

She turned when they reached her porch and held her hand out. "My phone, please."

Peter smirked and pulled her phone out, checking her screen. "Ah, you have several missed calls and texts."

Wendy grabbed the phone from Peter and unlocked it, then he snatched it back.

"Peter!" she shouted. "That's not yours." She reached for the phone, but his reflexes were too quick. He somehow managed to read the text even while moving the phone out of her reach.

When he finished, he narrowed his eyes at her, then thrust his hand forward, returning the phone between his fingers. "Who's Evan?"

Well, blast it all.

Wendy went for nonchalance. "He's the man I'm dating." She shrugged like it was no big deal.

"As in Evan Roberts, the fencing teacher?" Peter laughed without humor.

"The very one."

"You said you'd been 'reacquainted' with him—where do you know him from?"

Why does Peter even care?

Inwardly she huffed. She didn't want to see where this conversation would go.

"Peter, you know a lot of people and I know a lot of people." She glanced at her door and decided it was time for the evening to come to an end. She rushed through her next words. "It's late and I need to go inside. Thank you for a nice evening. Good night."

And though Peter could move at lightning speed, Wendy managed to slip inside and lock her door before he could even protest.

What a disaster, she thought. She leaned against the door and read Evan's message.

Evan: *Just want to make sure you're alright. I'm concerned since you weren't at class, and you didn't answer my calls. But I'll not miss our date this weekend. Text me when you get this.*

Her heart picked up speed as she read his message.

Wendy: *It's a long story. I can tell you more tomorrow. When should I be ready?*

Evan: *I'm anxious to see you. Is a breakfast date too early?*

Wendy: *9:30am?*

Evan: *You'll make me wait that long?*

Wendy chuckled and wrote back: *How about 9:00 instead? I might resemble a zombie if I don't get some sleep.*

Evan: *Even as a zombie, you'd radiate beauty and goodness.*

Wendy shook her head and smiled. He had such a way with words.

Evan: *But yes, I'll be at your door then.*

Wendy: *Across the street?*

Evan texted a winking emoji, and Wendy sighed. She could slip out without her brothers noticing who was at the door. And even if they saw him, Evan had changed. They might not even recognize him.

∞

Peter fumed all the way back to his car.

You think you can mess with people's emotions, Wendy's words echoed in his mind. Tessa had said something similar. *Where's your empathy, Peter? Do you really think others should change just to please you?*

Somewhere deep in Peter's conscience, the sensation of regret pushed its way to the surface. His pulse sped in panic as he desperately shoved it down—he wasn't in the wrong. But if that was the case, why did his chest ache? Why would two separate people give him the same message in chastisement?

Perhaps the world was against him. The sensation of regret seemed to shake its head doubtfully before Peter shoved it away. Yes, Wendy must be out to get him. All he'd done was give her a longed-for date. With a kiss at the end even.

How could she have rejected his kiss? He knew she'd wanted it for so long. And it was the final arsenal he'd been banking on to secure his place on her pedestal again. But it didn't work. It baffled him and wounded his pride and ego. He refused to believe he had lost her esteem, but he couldn't think of what else he could do to become number one in her mind again. Would his station in life never return to its former glory?

And what had he done to lose that spot in the first place? It couldn't have been his fault. It must be that blasted Evan Roberts. He'd turned Wendy's head and now Peter had lost Wendy's esteem. Just like he'd lost control over the rest of their group's esteem.

Not that he wanted a *relationship* with Wendy. This wasn't some love triangle. He just wanted her highest regard as he always had before.

Peter mechanically got into his car and started the engine. He was so lost in thought that he didn't notice the *p-thump p-thump* sound one of his tires made as he sped down the street. He made it halfway home before the unusual sound finally caught his attention. He pulled over, jumped out of the car with irritation, and noticed his back left tire was completely flat.

His tires had been fine all evening. Had he run over some piece of scrap metal on the way home? Or perhaps a nail? He bent down to inspect it.

Heat filled his face, and his mind filled with fury as his finger traced the long, clean gash in the tire. It was no accident—someone had slashed his tire. And since everything had worked properly up until he dropped off Wendy, it had most likely been slashed while he walked her to her door.

Truly, the world must be against him. But why did his conscience seem bent on disagreeing?

CHAPTER NINETEEN

Evan: *I'm here.*

      Wendy: *I'll be right down.*

Though sleep had been sparse, Wendy was up and ready for her date with Evan. She gathered her shoes from her closet and tip-toed downstairs to keep from waking John and Michael.

To her surprise, both were in the kitchen. And both turned her way as she tried to sneak to the front door.

"Hullo, Wendy," John said from the table. "You were out late last night."

"Yes," she said while coming up with a way to escape the topic.

Michael sat at the table. "What were you up to?" He spooned a bite of cereal.

"What were the two of you up to last night?" she asked curiously, turning the question around.

"Math," Michael said before becoming preoccupied with his bowl of cereal.

John shrugged. "Just meeting up with my new friend."

"And neither of you care to expound on any of that?" Wendy asked.

Michael shook his head as he stared at his bowl.

"Not really," John said, shrugging again.

If they wouldn't say any more, neither would Wendy. "Well then, I'm off for the morning. I'll see you both later."

Michael waved and John nodded.

Wendy's chest ached at the lack of communication. Their relationship had always been open, with each of them excited to share the happenings of their lives. But now everything was kept hidden, guarded by stilted answers and avoidance. Would their communication return to normal? Wendy sighed, realizing she could be the first to mend their broken connection. The right moment would come at some point.

She left the townhouse and crossed the quiet street to Evan's car. She peeked over her shoulder, making sure John and Michael weren't watching her, and slid into the passenger seat.

Evan as a fencing instructor was an impressive intimidation. Evan as an evening date was mysterious and alluring. But Evan in the daytime made Wendy's heart skip in an entirely new way. Who knew this former pirate had such casual charm, with his tousled hair in the morning sunlight and the graphic T-shirt that sat snug on his shoulder and chest muscles? And the way one corner of his mouth lifted as Wendy entered his Jeep had her toes curling in delight.

"Is it too early to kiss you?" he asked.

"Before we've eaten?" Wendy smirked.

Evan leaned over, caressed her neck with his left hand, and pulled her to him for the loveliest of kisses as the sunshine poured through the windshield. Wendy's eyelids stayed closed when he pulled back, embedding the moment into her memory.

Evan kissed the corner of her mouth. "Good morning," he whispered.

"Can it always stay like this?" she whispered back.

"What a lovely adventure that would be," Evan said as he ran his thumb down her face.

Wendy's stomach broke the moment as it demanded sustenance with a grumble. Her hand flew to her midsection. Blasted traitor.

Evan chuckled. "Let's go satisfy your need for food."

Wendy sighed. "If we must."

He took her to a breakfast-based restaurant that served everything from eggs benedict to waffles topped with fried chicken. The combined flavors of the latter had the most satisfactory result Wendy had ever tasted.

"So, what happened last night?" Evan asked after he'd finished his food.

Wendy sighed and lowered her fork. "Peter forced me on a date with him."

"Wouldn't that be considered kidnapping?" Evan asked with a smirk.

"Says the man who kidnapped plenty of people in a past life," Wendy said with raised eyebrows.

"That's unrelated. Tell me more."

She summed up the horrid experience as best she could, leaving out the kiss at the end as she wasn't sure how Evan would take that bit of information.

The retelling left her buzzing in agitation. Evan reached over and set his hand on hers. "I can tell this upset you. Let's distract you from the memory."

"What did you have in mind?"

His next destination surprised her as they pulled into the parking lot of the local zoo. The walking proved beneficial to settle her stomach, and the variety of animals astounded Wendy.

"I knew giraffes were tall," she mused, "but the height of a two-story building?"

"Come now," Evan countered. "You've flown higher than that."

Wendy tilted her head in consideration. "True. But the fact that an animal can grow to such a height is fascinating."

The crocodiles, though longer than thirteen feet, were less astounding to Wendy. "I've seen bigger," Wendy said, hiding a smile.

Evan shuddered and stayed several steps away from the enclosure. "Yes, and we know its favorite food."

Wendy's laugh had a few heads turning. "Yes, but it seems as though you've gotten over that situation well enough."

"I've had a rather pleasant distraction as of late." He wound his fingers through hers. "But I still don't want to look at them."

They strolled through the zoo, admiring the animals and taking pictures together. They covered nearly every exhibit, but Wendy refused to enter the reptile house.

"After what happened with the rattlesnake, I believe I've had enough slithering creatures for the entirety of my life." Her breathing became shallow as she recalled the incident in April, and her body began to shiver like a leaf in the breeze.

Evan pulled her into his arms, and she rested her head on his chest, matching her breaths with his and counting his heartbeats. Soon enough, her body and mind calmed, and the memory of the rattlesnake slipped to the back of her mind. Evan kissed the top of her head, and she savored the spot of warmth his lips left.

He insisted on walking her to her door when he brought her home, saying he wanted to be with her in case the snake memory surfaced at her front porch.

"Thank you," she said as they reached the top step. "Even if the memory did become a problem again, it's workable when you're here to steady me through it."

Evan raised an eyebrow. "Does this mean I get a good-night kiss?"

Wendy chuckled. "It's three in the afternoon."

"A mid-afternoon post-date kiss, then."

Wendy tilted her head upward and Evan met her halfway, setting her entire being ablaze with the wonders his lips did to hers. She moaned with pleasure and he pulled her closer.

So engrossed in Evan's kiss, Wendy failed to hear footsteps approach on the other side of the door until it was too late.

"Wendy, we heard voices. Is everything all right?" John asked.

Wendy, who faced the door, pulled back with wide eyes.

"Ah," John said with a knowing smile. "So this is the man who's caught your attention."

Wendy nodded, her eyes wide and her heart in her throat. She glanced at Evan, who faced the street, and willed him not to turn around. But he met her eyes, and his own seemed to imply that it was time to tell her brothers the truth.

Michael came behind John. "Is this her boyfriend then?" he asked, his voice laced with excitement.

Wendy shut her eyes and nodded to Evan. He touched her chin, and she opened her eyes to face the inevitable.

CHAPTER TWENTY

E van turned while wrapping his arm around Wendy's back, the gesture conveying his claim and support of Wendy, which she appreciated.

Both brothers stood frozen in shock at the sight of him. Michael's jaw dropped, and John's eyes had never seemed wider, even with the magnification his glasses had once given them.

Once the shock wore off, both went into the instinctive battle stance they'd had in Neverland, knees bent with their hands reaching for swords they hadn't carried for three years.

"Unhand her, you scoundrel!" John shouted.

Wendy shut her eyes and sighed. His overprotectiveness touched her heart but irritated her, nonetheless.

"John, he's not the same now," she said in a low voice.

John jutted an accusing finger at Evan. "Do you know who that is?" he shouted. "How can you defend him like that?"

"Must we have this discussion out in the open?" Wendy asked. She tugged Evan's arm and pulled him into her townhome, shutting the door behind him.

"Great," John yelled. "Now he knows where we live. He can slit our throats while we sleep. Nothing is safe anymore. I can't believe you didn't know who he was before you started dating him. I didn't take you for a fool, Wendy."

At that accusation, Wendy's irritation jumped to anger. Her expression must've matched her emotions, for both brothers stepped back with raised hands.

"How dare you question my sanity and intellect!" She stepped forward. "Have I ever given either of you a reason to doubt me?"

John and Michael shared a glance. "Other than this?" John gestured to Evan.

"*This* is Evan Roberts—" Wendy began.

"You mean Captain Hook," John countered.

"A pirate," Michael added.

"No, this is a changed man who left all that is bad behind him and accepted the chance at a new start. This is not the person you knew in Neverland. He's a *completely* different person."

"Well," John said, searching the room as though trying to grasp at anything to justify his position. "What about . . . Peter?"

"*Peter?*" Wendy and Michael asked in unison.

Evan turned his head away from Wendy, but she could hear his snicker.

"Yes, Peter." John crossed his arms, glowering at Wendy.

"What about him?" Wendy asked in confusion.

"Well, isn't he your hero—your love interest?"

"Peter?" Wendy shrugged. "Well, he's *Peter*. Immature, self-centered Peter."

"Isn't he anything to you?"

For goodness' sake, Wendy thought. *John is so desperate to take Evan out of the picture he's proposing Peter as a suitable substitute.* She rolled her eyes.

"Hmph," John exclaimed. "Eye rolling is unladylike, Wendy. It doesn't suit you."

John's ridiculous stance was too much. Wendy took a step toward him and rolled her eyes deliberately in his face.

John gasped. "You're worse than Tinkerbell."

"Oh, for goodness' sake," Wendy said, rolling her eyes again.

"Hook is a bad influence on you, Wendy," John warned.

"If Evan was still Hook, then that would be true," she answered. "But he's not. Not anymore."

"Why not Peter?" John grumbled.

"Honestly, John," Michael said, gesturing to Wendy. "I'm not keen on this revelation either. But Wendy's been on Peter's heels for years, and where has it gotten her? He's too much into himself to see her. And how would you actually feel if he started dating her? Do you see him giving her the attention and credit she deserves?"

John huffed a few times, then dropped his defensive position and let a long breath out. "You're right," he said. "He's not the sort of man we want for Wendy."

"Or the sort of man that *Wendy* wants for Wendy," Wendy said.

The brothers eyed Evan.

"How is he here, anyway?" John asked with a raised brow.

Wendy sighed and turned to Evan. "Would you share your story with them?"

He stood next to the door and explained his circumstances to John and Michael, the decision to leave piracy and his hook in Neverland, stowing away on the ship, separating from the group and making a new life for himself, and finally, discovering Wendy in his fencing class.

Michael eyed them both. "And he hasn't tried to kill you?"

Wendy nodded.

"And you've been seeing each other since then?" Michael continued.

Evan took her hand and laced his fingers between hers.

"Clearly, you believe him," Michael observed while eyeing their joined hands. "At least enough to pursue this."

John spoke up. "And without telling us about it one jot. What a secret to keep from your own brothers."

Wendy's eyes narrowed at him, causing him to flinch. "What secrets are *you* keeping, John? You've been out several nights each week without any explanation as to where you're going."

Just then the doorbell rang, and John's neck turned red as he pulled out his phone to check the time. "Blast," he whispered.

Michael moved to answer the door, but John put his arm out to stop him. "I'll get it." He pulled the door open only wide enough for him to exit through it, closing the door behind him.

Michael's eyebrows furrowed as he and Wendy exchanged glances. She nodded to the door, and Michael opened it, revealing John and Karmen on the front porch. John's hands were gesturing animatedly as he explained something.

Karmen leaned around him with wide eyes and her hand covered her mouth. John turned, taking in the fact that Wendy saw them both on the front porch.

Karmen dropped her hand. "We thought you'd be gone, chica."

Wendy stared, processing the scene. "This is your mystery man," she stated.

Karmen's head inched up and down in confirmation.

"And this," Wendy said to John, "is who you've been meeting with at night."

John sighed. "We were going to tell you—"

"John, what a hypocrite you are," Wendy said, raising her voice.

"I promise, it wasn't going to be a secret forever," he explained.

"And Karmen," Wendy turned to her friend. "How? Why?" She asked this last part with obvious confusion. Karmen could certainly attract several fine men, but *John*?

Karmen shrugged. "He's just so sweet. We met at the nursing school graduation, remember?"

"How long has this been happening?" Wendy asked.

"About a week before the fencing class." Karmen pressed her lips in before continuing. "I'm so sorry, amiga. I wanted him all to myself before telling you. I love it when he talks nerdy to me."

John's face pinked, but he made no denial.

Wendy nodded and went back in the house, the slightest bit disturbed imagining John saying anything to stir romantic feelings in Karmen. But also relieved she wasn't the only one in a secret relationship.

"What about you, Michael?" Wendy addressed him. "How many math assignments can you have in a week? You've been at Emily's nearly every evening. You have secrets of your own, it would seem."

As though on cue, the doorbell rang again. Michael scrunched his eyes closed and blew out a breath before answering the door. Emily stood on the porch, holding a set of papers.

She scanned the group before addressing Michael with a shy smile. "You left this last night." Michael took them, glancing back at the group inside.

Wendy eyed the papers. "Math homework?"

Emily sent Wendy a confused expression as John swiped the papers from Michael.

"John, wait," Michael protested.

"Is this sheet music?" John asked in disbelief. He held the papers in front of him. "What sort of song is this?"

Michael swiped the papers back as Emily's eyes scanned the group. "It's alternative. Michael plays the keyboard." She turned her eyes to Michael, a question in her eyes.

Michael shut his eyes in defeat. "They don't know."

"Oh." Emily's eyes widened. "I'm sorry, I thought you told them."

"Told us what?" John inserted. Wendy was just as curious.

Emily's mouth opened and closed before answering. "We formed a band with some friends. We practice after dinner at my house."

Evan leaned in, whispering for only Wendy's ears. "Seems he's been studying something after all."

Wendy's heart relaxed at Evan's lightness, and her anger at her brothers' accusations and hypocrisy dissolved. The matter had been addressed, they'd each been called out on their clandestine behavior, and now was the time to bring together what had been pulled apart.

Wendy took a fortifying breath, owning her choices. "I'm sorry for keeping this a secret." She lifted hers and Evan's joined hands. "I was scared I wouldn't have your support. You're both so protective."

John sighed. "I'm sorry too. I don't even have a good excuse."

All eyes turned to Michael. "Likewise. I was nervous about my part in a band."

"He's really good," Emily supplied.

"Yes, he's played the piano for years," Wendy said, remembering days long ago listening to Michael as a young boy practicing the piano for hours in their music room.

Silence hung for what seemed like an hour, though it was perhaps only a minute.

"So," John said, jutting his thumb toward the door. "We're going to leave now."

"And I have actual math homework I need to complete," Michael added.

Wendy gestured to her brothers and they gathered in a hug, much like the hugs they'd given perhaps thousands of times to each other. Hugs of trust and support. Wendy's heart expanded at the love she had for her brothers and the relief she felt at their secrets ending. She went up on tiptoes to kiss their cheeks. "Thank you for understanding," she whispered before glancing back at Evan.

"This will take some time to wrap my head around," Michael confessed in a whisper as his eyes sought Evan behind her.

"Likewise," John added while scowling.

"But your support?" Wendy asked them.

They both nodded, unspoken words of acceptance and love conveyed in the simple gesture.

They filed out of the house, John and Karmen leaving first, with Emily offering to help Michael with his math assignment. Which left Wendy and Evan alone to convey their farewells to each other in several blissful moments, wrapped in each other's arms.

CHAPTER TWENTY-ONE

P eter wasn't angry because he had to change his flat tire. He wasn't angry because he had to pay a pretty penny to replace it. He wasn't angry because of the inconvenience these things caused. He could handle all those things.

What made him angry was that someone had intentionally slashed his tire right under his nose. He wasn't accustomed to being the brunt of mischief—he was used to being the one to inflict it.

It festered in him all weekend. And all the week after. His mind was only half present during work, his mood brooding and antisocial, atypical of his usual confident, flirtatious, and cocky attitude. Tessa cast him angry glances at the beginning of the week. But by Thursday, her expression held concern.

Why would she care? He didn't need anyone's help.

On Friday he called in sick to work and escaped into the mountains. Nature called to him—it calmed him.

He hiked to a camp ground and away from people. Stupid people. People who rejected and judged him. People who slashed his tires. People who refused to think highly of him. He was a hero, after all.

He'd done so much to earn people's good opinions. If he wasn't a hero and a leader, who was he?

With his tent up and a campfire burning lively before him, he sat on the leaf-strewn ground and set his thoughts and feelings free. He let the emotions surge full force through his mind and body. He heaved a breath, closed his eyes, and curled his hands around the dirt and flora next to him. He dropped his head to his chest and wished he could fly away from it all. He sacrificed everything to come to Reality.

What am I doing here? he wondered. *Why did I ever leave Neverland? What's my purpose in this place and time?* He let the questions ebb and flow, whispers of answers forming here and there.

I wanted to have a new adventure, he answered himself. *I didn't want to be left behind—everyone else was leaving. Wendy, John, Michael, the Lost Boys. I didn't want to miss out.*

But everyone else started to move on soon after they landed. They didn't need him as their leader now, and the pedestal he'd stood on for so long had eroded. The descent from the top left an agonizing void in his soul.

A tear escaped his eye, rolled down his face, and landed on the ground. He focused on the spot, then swiped the residual wetness from his face.

As the daylight faded, he climbed into his tent, slipped into his sleeping bag, curled into himself, and fell asleep.

He dreamed he was back in Neverland. But he sensed he was the only person on the island. No natives, no pirates, no mermaids, no Lost Boys, no allies or foes. Just him.

Then he heard a faint sound—a steady rhythm—approaching. He soon recognized it as a tick-tock. The only thing in Neverland that made that sound was the ginormous crocodile he'd fed Hook's hand to. But there was no Hook, so why would the crocodile bother coming ashore? The sound intensified, but he couldn't see the source anywhere.

Fear mounted in his heart from the unseen threat. He jumped to fly, but landed back on the ground. He climbed high into a nearby tree instead to avoid danger. The ticking was nearly deafening by that point, but still Peter could see nothing of the croc.

Then the sand below the tree moved, vibrating and shaking as though an isolated earthquake were happening in front of him.

The croc pushed its way out of the sand headfirst. The beast was just as massive as he remembered. It stretched at least forty feet long with sharp, pointed teeth poking out from its mouth, bright green scaly skin, a wide belly splayed over the sand, and four lazy looking limbs (which moved swifter than they appeared).

The croc flicked its tail and snapped its eyes straight up at Peter. The ticking suddenly stopped, but Peter's heart pounded. The croc narrowed its eyes at him, as though assessing Peter.

Peter couldn't stand the tension and terror, and he called out to the croc. "What do you want?"

He searched frantically left and right for some sort of escape—he'd always been able to fly away from it. But he was trapped up in the tree with the croc below. If he tried to run, he'd be caught for sure.

The croc shook its head in response to Peter's question.

"Gah," Peter screamed in alarm. Could the thing really understand what he said? If it did, why wouldn't it leave him be? "Shoo! Get away. No Hook here to eat." He shooed the croc with one hand, temporarily losing his balance.

The croc shook its head again.

Peter's fear shifted to irritation at not being obeyed. Why would no one do as he wished they would—in Reality or in this dream?

"Are you mocking me?" he shouted at it.

But the croc shook its head again.

What sort of miscommunication was this? Peter realized that if it really wanted to eat him, it would've taken aggressive action by that point.

Peter regarded the croc, squinting. "Are you even trying to eat me?"

It shook its head.

Peter's level of fear dropped several degrees, but if the croc wasn't going to eat him, then what did it want? "Hook's not here, it's just me. Are you looking for him?"

Another head shake from the croc. Peter chewed on this answer before addressing it again. "Where is Hook? Did you eat him after I left?"

Another head shake.

Peter muttered a curse and turned back to the croc. "Well, then where'd he go?"

This time it directed its eyes upward.

"Up?" Peter asked with confusion.

It nodded, then looked up again.

Peter followed its gaze and saw his ship—the flying one they'd taken to leave Neverland. He stared at it in disbelief. That ship had crashed with irreparable damage when they'd landed in Reality, so what was it doing here?

He saw two figures aboard the deck. The first he immediately recognized as Wendy. She gazed up at a dark-haired figure. A second later he recognized the other person as Hook himself.

"Hook's on my ship," Peter pointed. "What's he doing on my ship?"

The croc simply looked back up at the ship.

What Peter saw next nearly made him fall from the tree. Hook was kissing Wendy, and she was kissing him back.

Despair filled his whole body like weights. Losing his friend to his enemy? What sort of betrayal was this? How could she do this to him?

"I don't deserve that!" he shouted at the croc, pointing to the scene above. Rather than move its head this time, the croc rolled its eyes.

Peter reared back. "Oh, you think I deserve this, do you? What did I do?"

The croc blinked, turned around, and ambled away.

"Wait," Peter called. "Answer me. What did I do? What's happening?"

The croc didn't answer as it made its way to the water's edge, slipped into the sea, and disappeared under the water.

Peter returned his attention to where the ship had been, but it was gone. He was alone again.

What did I do to lose a friend to an enemy?

"Peter?"

Hearing his name woke Peter from his dream. Sweat dampened his body, and his head pounded. He put his hand to his head and groaned. He reached for his water bottle and took a sip to clear his mind.

"Peter? Are you okay? Can I come in?"

Tessa? What was she doing here?

Peter scrambled out of his sleeping bag and unzipped the tent. Tessa knelt outside, a backpack on her back and a flashlight in her hand.

His heart picked up speed. Was he dreaming still?

"What're you doing here?" he asked, genuinely curious.

She bit her lower lip. "You haven't been yourself this week. I kinda followed you here."

His head pulled back. "Why?"

"I wanted to make sure you're okay."

"After what I did to you?"

She shrugged. "You've obviously got some problems."

Peter scowled.

"I didn't know if you were unstable as well as narcissistic." Tessa glanced around his camp area with her flashlight. "This is a nice spot."

"I'm not unstable. I just needed to get away for a while."

"You were moaning a few minutes ago."

Peter rolled his eyes. "I was asleep. It was a bad dream." Bad, confusing, disturbing, and frightening. Peter replayed the image of Wendy and Hook in each other's arms and rage threatened to burst from every inch of his skin.

Tessa must have sensed his animosity. "I hope you're not mad I came. My parents would do some stupid things when they were upset, and I didn't want to see that happen to you with your disorder."

"I don't have a disorder, Tessa." Really, must she continue to bring this up?

"That's what narcissists do—they deny they have a problem."

He huffed. "I'm fine. See?" He spread his arms out. "All in one piece. No damage. You can go now." He reached out to zip the tent closed, signifying his wish for Tessa to leave.

She stopped his hand. "What happened in the dream?"

He scowled. "You're not my therapist. You're not even *a* therapist."

Tessa's jaw clenched. "You need to get one. I've seen lives go from bad to worse with this mindset you have, Peter. I'm not going to watch from the sidelines while another person screws up their life by clinging to narcissism. It's toxic." She moved her way into his tent, much to his surprise. "Now, tell me about the dream. Talking helps with processing."

Rather than describe the scene from his unconscious images, he gave a general description. "I was alone until a beast came and mocked me with its eyes and then I found out someone I thought was my friend betrayed me. Then you woke me up. Can I go back to sleep now?"

Tessa regarded him with hardened eyes. "Maybe everyone's right about you."

"What do you mean?"

"They said you're self-seeking, arrogant, and a total player. I told people what you did to me. I was willing to defend you, thinking there was some hope for you to work through this. They told me you were a lost cause and that I should stop trying to help you." She shifted her way toward the tent opening. "They were right. I wasted my time trying to help you. But you can't help someone who refuses to see the truth." She shimmied out the tent door.

"Tessa, wait." Peter called. He heard her retreating footsteps in the underbrush, then silence.

Ugh, girls were so ridiculous. She'd followed him out here to save him from himself? What rubbish. Peter was the one to save others. She really had wasted her time coming up here to help him.

He set himself back in the sleeping bag and his thoughts took over.

She wanted to analyze the dream. Silly girl. Peter had probably just eaten something random that didn't agree with him. Not all dreams held significance.

And Hook and Wendy . . . of all the ridiculous notions. He huffed a laugh, mocking the idea. His sweet and innocent friend Wendy falling prey to the enemy? Good thing they left Hook in Neverland.

His thoughts turned to the truthfulness of his situation. His friends were thriving without him, and he resented it. Wendy was dating someone, which he also resented.

Peter's conscience had never been something he'd listened to, as he'd always forced it away to keep guilt out of his life. But in his vulnerable state, the emotion sprouted and demanded attention.

Tessa's words rolled through his mind.

You're self-seeking, arrogant, and a total player. I told people what you did to me . . . They told me you were a lost cause and that I should stop trying to help you.

He didn't need anyone to save him. He was grand exactly the way he was.

That's what narcissists do—they deny they have a problem.

Tessa's words struck him. Was he denying it, or was the rest of the world simply wrong about him? Maybe he was a misunderstood hero. But if that were the case, why had the guilt begun to press through him?

I'm not going to watch from the sidelines while another person screws up their life by clinging to narcissism. It's toxic.

Peter rubbed his arm. Tessa had cared.

They told me you were a lost cause.

Peter swallowed, the movement feeling like sand in his throat. Was he truly such an awful person that he'd driven his friends away from him?

He reflected on his interactions with them recently.

He'd shut Thomas's comments down impatiently at the campout. Then there was the rubber snake at his last meetup with Wendy. And then the real snake—he cringed at the memory of her terror as he watched her from the sidelines. Then he'd forced her on a date and kissed her without her consent. He shut his eyes and pulled his lips in.

And Tessa. What a horrible thing he'd put her through, toying with her emotions and then dropping her coldly, all because he'd made it a game to do so. His throat constricted remembering the moment her face fell at his confession.

His guilt stretched wide with each memory and weighed on him heavier than his ship.

"Is this what I did to drive them away? Is this what I did to deserve that wretched dream?" He stared at his hands.

His knee-jerk reaction to subdue culpability kicked in. No one was perfect. His friends had done things he didn't like, either. The blame couldn't fall completely on him.

But at the same time, he hated the lack of connection with the others and the distance between them. He didn't want things to remain as they were. He'd been trying to establish himself as their leader and hero again, but had failed.

Where did that leave him?

He thought of Wendy, Tessa, and even Tink. He'd left her in Neverland intentionally, deceptively.

He laid down again from the intensity of guilt, which pressed down as though the croc itself were sprawled over him.

Tessa's comment about a therapist came to his mind.

You ought to get one. I've seen lives go from bad to worse with this mindset you have, Peter.

Did he want help? Could he get help? He sat back up and wondered who he would be without the cocky, self-assured attitude he wore everywhere he went, around everyone he met. He stared at the tent door and asked himself, "Am I still myself if I change? Do I lose my identity?"

Movement within the tent caught his eye and he startled. His Neverland shadow waved at him from the tent wall, replacing the Reality one that had been there a second ago.

"Where've you been for the last three years?" he demanded. "How did you even get here?"

It pointed toward the tent door and Peter huffed. "Not this again. You know I can't always figure out what you're trying to tell me."

It set its hands on its hips and leaned its head to the side.

"First the croc in my dream and now you." Peter's head tilted back as he gave in. "Fine, I'll try to guess."

The shadow clapped its hands then pointed to the tent door again.

"You want me to leave?" Peter guessed. His shadow shook its head, then pointed to Peter and mimicked talking with its hand.

"You heard me talking?"

His shadow nodded with a thumbs-up then pointed outside again.

"You heard me talking and you want me to go outside." Head shake. "You want me to go away? Go up, down, sideways?"

His shadow made a gesture as though to hit Peter upside the head, which made him chuckle. "You can't touch me here, can you?" It tossed its hands up before indicating continuing the guessing game.

"Okay, so not out, up, down, sideways. What about through, over, backward, forward—"

It held its hand up as though to stop him from guessing.

"Forward. You want me to move forward?"

It made jazz-hands, confirming Peter's guess.

"Like with Tessa's suggestion about a therapist? You probably heard her say that."

It nodded.

"So, move forward and see a therapist. Do you think that'll help?"

It gave a thumbs-up.

"Why're you here, anyway? And why are you choosing now to intervene? This would've been helpful a while ago. Things are a mess with everyone."

It held its hands out in surrender. Then it glanced left and right before waving goodbye, leaving Peter with his Reality shadow again in the tent.

He touched the tent wall. Was he delusional? He shook his head and lay down on his sleeping bag.

Move forward. He pictured himself accepting his friends' independence and respecting them as equals. He pictured Wendy's bright smile as he behaved as a gentleman when in her company. His muscles relaxed, and his mind cleared of the misery he'd felt mere minutes before.

He put his hands behind his head. Thoughts and ideas of change and reconciliation kept him up for hours. At some point during his musings, he fell back asleep. This time with no dreams.

CHAPTER TWENTY-TWO

Around seven-thirty in the morning, there was a knock on the Darling siblings' door. Wendy, who stood in the kitchen surveying breakfast cereal options, answered the door, wondering who would visit this early on Memorial Day weekend.

Her eyes widened, surprised to see Coby on their doorstep.

"Coby, what a lovely surprise. Come in."

He stayed in the doorway, biting his lower lip.

"Wendy, who is it?" John's voice echoed.

"It's Coby. Come downstairs," Wendy called out.

John and Michael trotted down a moment later.

Coby took in each of the siblings, one at a time, landing back on Wendy's face. "You guys aren't gonna believe this, but he's here."

"Who's here, Coby?" John asked.

"Hook," Coby answered. "Hook's *here*. I've been working with him for, like, a year. Only he's not Hook. He's ..."

"He's Evan," Wendy filled in. Her mind reeled—Coby had been working with Evan? And neither had recognized the other? How had they finally realized what was going on?

Coby turned to Wendy. "You knew?"

Wendy nodded. "Yes. Though John and Michael only recently found out."

John cast her a disapproving glare, to which Wendy rolled her eyes. "How is it that you and Evan only just put the connection together?"

Coby ran his hand over the side of his face. "We got to talking about how he'd reconnected with 'an old friend' and started dating her. I thought it was cool how we both know a Wendy. But it was the same Wendy. And he asked where I came from, so I told him we all came from Neverland—"

"And he believed you?" John interrupted.

"John." Michael elbowed him.

"Sorry," John said.

"So, yeah, he believed me, and we talked about it after work. Then it was like—" He made an explosion sound while splaying his hands above his head with wide eyes. "I think he didn't recognize me because, you know, I'm all grown up now. And I don't talk with the accent like the rest of you guys. I guess it makes sense."

John shook his head. "But then, how did *you* not recognize him? He sounds much the same and looks much the same. Well, minus the hook."

Coby pondered his answer. "I think it was one of those out-of-context things, you know? I didn't expect to see him here. And he doesn't act anything like the Captain Hook we knew from before."

John raised an eyebrow. "The verdict on his trustworthiness has yet to be decided."

"Dude," Coby said, frowning at John. "He's a good guy now. Nothing like before."

John folded his arms. "If you say so."

Coby turned to Wendy. "Does Peter know he's here?"

Wendy shook her head. "I don't believe so. If he did, we would know."

"That's gonna be a pain." Coby shook his head.

"What do you mean, 'going to be'?" John asked.

Coby looked at the siblings. "Well, he's gonna find out, don't you think? I mean, Evan's dating Wendy."

"He makes a good point." Wendy tapped a finger to her mouth.

John surveyed the group. "Perhaps he'll take the news better than we anticipate. What's the worst that could happen?"

❧

Wendy's stomach growled as she shut the door after Coby's visit.

"Time for breakfast," John said. "Michael and I will make something this morning. Won't we, Michael?" He turned to his brother for confirmation. Michael wore a mix of doubt and amusement on his face.

"*We* are going to make something?" he asked John. "Or *Michael* is going to make something? We all know you're a disaster in the kitchen, John. No offense meant." He patted John on the shoulder.

John heaved a sigh. "None taken. I guess you're on breakfast duty then." He put one hand on Michael's arm and indicated toward the kitchen with the other. The scent of French toast and scrambled eggs soon filled their home.

Once breakfast was ready, the siblings sat at the kitchen table and ate in silence for several minutes.

"Michael, you've outdone yourself," Wendy said, indicating to her nearly empty plate.

Michael smiled and nodded.

John, however, had other things on his mind. "Why Evan?" he asked baldly.

Wendy stopped eating, her forkful of eggs halfway to her mouth.

"Glad you like breakfast, too, John," Michael teased.

"Yes, yes, Michael. It's wonderful. It always is." He shot his brother an annoyed look and Michael smirked back.

Wendy laughed and continued to eat.

"I'm not joking," John said. "You could have any bloke around. You could even have Peter if he'd shape up a bit."

"That's a big *if*," Michael said.

John ignored him. "So why Evan?"

"You know she's meeting up with him later, right?" Michael supplied.

John swatted his hand at Michael. "Shush. I want her to answer the question."

Wendy took a breath, collecting her thoughts. She then launched into the events of Peter's impromptu date. The way he tricked her into missing class, the argument in the restaurant parking lot, his tenuous attention at dinner, and Peter's kiss when he dropped her off at home.

Michael's eyes widened. "He *kissed* you?"

"Haven't you wanted him to do that since, well, forever?" John asked.

"Yes." Wendy shrugged. "For years. But he's been the same since we came here."

She shook her head, contradicting herself. "No, he's actually gotten worse since we came here. He's grown quite handsome, which is obvious to any girl. And he knows that. And he uses his charm and charisma to his advantage every chance he has." She felt tears prick the corners of her eyes. "He flirts with any woman he wants when I'm there with him. Like I don't matter. Or rather as though I only matter when he desires my attention to give his massive ego a boost." She slumped in her chair.

Wendy saw her brothers share a look of worry between each other. Michael put his hand on Wendy's arm. "We didn't know he affected you so deeply in such a negative way," he said gently.

"It's no wonder you didn't want him to kiss you after behaving like such a blighter. I'd have pushed him away too." John sat back and folded his arms.

Wendy bit down on her smile while sharing a look with Michael. John must have realized how his statement sounded and put his hands in front of him. "Not like *that*," he amended. "What I mean is that if a girl treated me the way Peter treated Wendy, then went so far as to kiss me as though all was dandy between us..."

Wendy stifled a laugh and patted him on the back. "We understand you, John."

He rolled his eyes, which elicited a snort-laugh from Michael, which sent Wendy into a fit of giggles.

John huffed. "You're both astronomically immature."

Wendy burst out laughing while Michael continued to snort-laugh.

John huffed again and stood from the table. "Let's get the kitchen cleaned up, shall we? Why are you both still laughing? Don't you have something better to do? *Honestly.*"

Chapter Twenty-three

L ater that morning, Evan waited on a wooden bench for Wendy at a nearby park while enjoying the sunshine. He crossed one ankle over his knee, leaned his head against the back of the bench to feel the sun on his face, and folded his hands behind his head. His fingers ran over the surface of his recent haircut, done in fashion with the current style. He wondered what Wendy would think of it.

A shadow suddenly blocked the sun from his face. He opened his eyes, and his heart thumped against his ribs. The sight of Wendy above him, illuminated by the sunlight behind her like an angel, was absolutely captivating.

He smiled up at her, and she smiled back with a whispered, "Hullo there."

They'd been together only a short time, but he'd known her for so long. He admired her strength in mind, body, and spirit. He'd seen the care she'd given her brothers, the Lost Boys, and even the undeserving Peter. He'd seen her grow from a sweet girl into this phenomenal woman before him.

The realization hit him like a cannonball smashing into a ship—he loved Wendy. How long he'd loved her, he couldn't determine, but he knew it now.

He stood and went around the bench to her, pulling her toward him. Their foreheads met in the middle, heat emanating between them.

Then Evan reached his hand behind Wendy's neck to pull her to him. Their lips met gently at first. Then it was Wendy whose lips urged his on. Her hands went behind his head, threading her fingers through his hair.

She stopped their kiss short with a gasp. "Your hair."

He pulled her back to him. "Never mind that," he murmured.

She willingly obeyed and his lips were on hers again. His pulse went erratic in his chest, like a sail snapping in a furious wind.

They pulled away from each other, each breathing deeply, with Wendy's hands clasped behind his head. Their noses touched, and he whispered her name. She bit her lower lip as she smiled.

Evan groaned longingly and pulled her to his mouth again, their kiss unrestrained. His mouth moved from her lips, and he trailed kisses down her chin to her throat, then he made his way back to her eager lips again.

Wendy exhaled a shaky breath as his hand slid up and down her neck. He could feel her tempestuous pulse pound against his fingers.

Then his hand caressed her face, making its way through her soft hair, and landing in her hand, fitting her delicate fingers between his.

"What a lovely way to begin our date," Wendy breathed.

"What happened after *your* date with Peter the other night?" he asked.

She scrutinized his face. "Why the sudden interest? I thought we left that discussion at the restaurant last week."

He tugged her hand, and they began a stroll around the park. "Mere curiosity."

"Is there something you need to tell *me* about what happened after my date with Peter?" she asked, lifting one corner of her mouth.

Evan chuckled. "Let's just say I stuck around after he brought you home ..."

Understanding hit and she glared at him. "You were there? Then you saw Peter walk with me to my apartment."

He bit back a smile. "Indeed."

"So, you saw how he took my phone from me."

"Blasted immature of him to do so," Evan observed.

"His curiosity seems to compel him to act before thinking," Wendy said. She paused before her hand flew to her mouth. "Oh!" she exclaimed. She stared at Evan while blushing.

She blushed like that the first time I captured her after she returned to Neverland.

"What has you turning red, Wendy?" he asked, smirking.

She lowered her hands. "You saw Peter kiss me," she whispered.

Evan's amusement fled and his mood darkened. "Yes. My instinct told me to pummel that blackguard to a pulp. Instead, I shouted and kicked a trash can to the other side of the street."

Wendy's eyes widened. "That's what that crashing sound was."

Evan wasn't finished. "It took every atom of self-control I had to not run over to him and ..." His chest tensed at the memory. "That pig-headed, selfish mongrel." He took a deep breath to calm himself and cleared his throat, scowling. "Yes, I saw him kiss you."

Wendy sighed. "He *was* pig-headed and selfish. I didn't want him to kiss me. As much as I thought I had wanted him to at one point. I'm amazed you didn't do something rash."

Evan's amusement returned and he remained silent, attempting to appear as the epitome of innocence. He focused on a tree nearby. Wendy moved her head into his line of sight. "Evander Roberts."

He turned back to her, eyebrows raised. "What?"

"*Did* you do something rash to him?" she asked.

"Well," he said, tilting his head. "Not precisely *to* him."

"What do you mean, *not precisely*?"

His mouth quirked into a poorly concealed smile. "Let's just say he likely had a floppy ride home."

Wendy's jaw dropped. "Did you slash his tires?"

"Just one," he clarified. "One singular tire. That's all."

Wendy blinked, then shook her head and blew out a heavy breath. "I suppose that response is preferable over physical violence."

"I quite agree." The satisfaction of slashing Peter's tire would last Evan a lifetime.

"Why did you leave the hook behind?"

"An interesting topic to bring up."

"As was asking about my date with Peter so you could tell me about his tire." Wendy nudged him with her arm.

"Fair enough," Evan said while chuckling. He raised his right arm, examining the stump where his hook used to be. "I didn't want it with me when I left."

"Why?" Wendy asked.

Evan glanced briefly at a nearby playground dappled in shade, contemplating his answer before turning to Wendy. "Too many memories connected to it. Things I didn't want to be associated with. It's the object that inspired fear in the inhabitants of Neverland. I don't want to inspire fear."

"What do you want to inspire now?" Wendy asked as they turned a corner at the edge of the park.

"A new start."

Wendy nodded. "Something we all came here for."

"Truly," he agreed. "So, no more hook for me."

Wendy turned to Evan, her mouth tilting up on one side. "So, as far as villainy is concerned, you're *off the hook*."

Evan laughed, tossing his head back. Then he swung her into his arms and kissed her breathless, sending fire racing through his entire body.

CHAPTER TWENTY-FOUR

Later that day Wendy and Evan entered her townhome to find John and Karmen on the couch playing video games.

"You bested me again," John said, thumping his controller on his legs. Wendy inwardly laughed at the pout on his face.

"No, you let me win." Karmen straightened when she noticed Wendy and Evan. "Hey! How was your morning?"

Michael entered the room. "I'm sure they were absolutely *hooked* on the scenery."

Wendy and Evan burst out laughing while John scowled and Karmen appeared confused.

"Does this mean you're warming up to our situation?" Wendy asked, lifting her and Evan's joined hands.

Michael shrugged. "I'd rather laugh about it than be angry. Wouldn't you, John?"

John grunted, then began another round of video games with Karmen.

"Speaking of scenery, we should go outside today," Karmen said as she obliterated John in the game.

Michael brightened. "A hike would be nice, especially after taking all those final exams last week. What a bludgeon they were."

"Sounds like you worked hard, Michael," Wendy said. She'd seen him study night after night leading up to the end of school.

"Well, you know what they say about work and play," Michael said as he texted someone.

Wendy grinned. "What do they say, Michael?"

He looked up from his phone and gave her a suppressed smile. "Work like a captain, play like a pirate."

"That's not *funny*, Michael," John protested over the sound of Evan's laugh.

"I'll see if Emily can join us." Michael went back to his phone.

Karmen clapped as she won the video game. "Isn't he so sweet to let me win again?" She leaned over and patted John's thigh.

John's eyes widened at her gesture and his sour demeanor brightened. "Of course, my dear. I'll let you win every time. Anything for your happiness."

Emily arrived at their door a moment later with a full backpack. "Water and sunscreen for the hike," she explained.

"I suppose that means we're going hiking," Evan observed.

"Where should we go?" Karmen asked, pulling her long, dark hair into a ponytail.

Michael piped up. "There's Outdoor Adventure Trek. They have some impressive hikes with tour guides. We went there for a field trip this past year. I ran into Peter, he works there—oh." He pursed his lips. "I forgot he works there. We can go elsewhere."

John swatted his arm. "It's a holiday—they're probably not even open. I say we go there and hike one of their public trails. No danger, see?"

Karmen said Peter's name and let loose a slew of Spanish. From the murderous look on Karmen's face, Wendy guessed they were words Karmen's mother would be ashamed to hear her say. Wendy's heart warmed just the same at her friend's defensiveness.

John's arm went around Karmen. "You're adorable when you're angry." She then purred several Spanish phrases that turned John's cheeks pink when he smiled.

Evan nudged Wendy's arm and snickered. "Are you following this?"

"You speak Spanish? I have no idea what she's saying," Wendy admitted.

Evan paused. "On second thought, perhaps you're best left in the dark. Too many innuendos."

Wendy was suddenly grateful she didn't speak Spanish. "Will you be able to contain yourself if Peter happens to be there?"

Evan shrugged. "I can handle seeing Peter. I've done it before. I can do it again."

"Yes," Wendy smirked. "Tires and all that."

Evan chuckled.

Wendy sighed and stood. "Shall we be off?"

She rode with Evan in his Jeep, and her brothers and Karmen rode with Emily in her car. They pulled in next to each other in the dirt-packed parking lot and John rolled down his window.

"It appears they're open after all. Maybe Peter's in there." He pointed to the cabin. Michael swatted John's arm. "What?"

"I'll see if he's working." Wendy headed into the cabin, where a handful of hikers and tour guides came and went. Rather than examine each individual to find Peter, she approached a guide. "Excuse me?"

The guide turned to Wendy with an open smile. "Hey, I'm Tessa. How can I help you?"

"I wondered if Peter is at work today."

Tessa's smile faltered. "Not yet, his shift starts later. Did you need him for something?"

"No, I was simply checking. Thank you." Wendy turned to go as a group of hikers entered the building.

"You guys, be careful," one of them yelled, drawing everyone's attention. "We saw rattlesnakes out there."

Snakes. Wendy's breathing grew shallow, and her balance teetered. Tessa caught her arm. "Are you okay? You're really pale. Here." She pulled a chair out for Wendy as the hikers showed everyone pictures of the rattlesnakes.

"Hang on," Tessa said as she saw the photos. "These aren't rattlesnakes. They're just gopher snakes." She proceeded to explain the mimicry of gopher snakes to fool predators into mistaking them for rattlesnakes. She went to the office computer and pulled up images of rattlesnakes versus gopher snakes. The likeness was uncanny.

But rather than be impressed at the ingenuity of the reptile, Wendy's thoughts went back to the incident on her front porch in April.

"You say they're harmless," she said to Tessa.

"Mm-hm. But they want you to think they're dangerous. They can even make a rattling sound." She played a video depicting the phony rattle of a gopher snake.

Wendy's jaw dropped. "Are they likely to be found in the city?"

Tessa shook her head, frowning. "I haven't really heard of any wandering into developed areas. The ones here seem to prefer the wilderness. Why do you ask?"

"Mere curiosity."

Tessa's mouth lifted in a gentle smile. "The next tour starts in about fifteen minutes, and we'll be avoiding any areas where snakes have been reported."

Wendy nodded, then left the cabin with her heart in her feet. Had Peter staged a rescue on April 1st? What was the likelihood that a harmless snake sat coiled on her porch and that Peter just happened to be nearby to catch her as she fainted so he could rid her porch of the creature? The odds seemed unlikely. Had he manipulated her in her weakness?

She shook the thoughts aside. She hadn't any proof that he'd done such a thing with those intentions.

"He's not here," she told the group as they rolled down their windows. "The next tour starts soon."

A curious group of hikers filed out of the building, a motley crew dressed in medieval attire and hiking boots.

Evan took her hand, threading his fingers through hers. "You seem out of sorts," he whispered as they entered the building. "What happened?"

"I'll explain once we're on the trail."

Tessa had the group sign waivers and pay the tour fee. Then another guide flagged Tessa with his hand. "FYI—That last group left their swords," he told her while pointing to a door that read "Storage". "The swords are locked up back there. Hopefully the group comes back for them soon."

"Swords?" John exclaimed.

"Why did they have swords?" Karmen asked the guide.

He shrugged. "They're just wooden ones. The group was doing some sort of medieval society activity and wanted to reenact a battle scene in the mountains. But we had them leave them here for their hike."

"Understandable," John said.

"And they forgot them?" Karmen asked with a confused expression. "How do you forget something like that?"

The guide shrugged, and Wendy and the others followed as Tessa led them through a side door, down a wood-lined path, and up a tree-covered trail into the hills beyond.

"Tell me what happened," Evan prompted Wendy as they took the end of the line.

Wendy reminded him of the snake incident from the first of April, then expounded on the revelation about rattlesnakes and gopher snakes. "They're nearly identical. The gopher snake even mimics the rattlesnake sound to ward off predators."

"You think it was a gopher snake on your porch?"

"I do. I also wonder how it got there, and I have my own theory." She explained her thoughts of Peter's involvement, given his flair for heroics and mischief.

"What a prank to play on you, preying on your fear of snakes." Evan's face darkened.

"I don't know for certain though."

"Still, it's absolutely the sort of horrid thing he would do. I only wonder why he'd choose you as his victim."

"Who knows?" Wendy let it drop as they followed Tessa along the hike.

Tessa led them past an open meadow brimming with wildflowers, a series of waterfalls of varying heights, through a shallow cave that smelled of sulfur, and through a thicket of evergreen trees.

Emily stopped at each location, taking several pictures and videos.

Michael sidled next to Wendy. "She wants to be a professional photographer someday."

Wendy's eyebrows rose. "She's a band member, a math tutor, *and* a photographer. A woman of many talents."

"That she is," Michael said, his softened eyes directed at Emily.

Wendy nudged his arm, and he responded with a smirk. "We're only friends."

"Of course," Wendy said with exaggerated sobriety.

John had asked if he could pick wildflowers at the meadow, but Tessa turned down the request. "Our rule is to take nothing but pictures and leave nothing but footprints."

"Ooh," Karmen marveled. "Clever slogan."

John leaned next to Karmen, and Wendy heard him mutter, "I wanted to make you a flower crown."

Karmen answered in Spanish, likely a compliment, eliciting a proud smile from John. He took her hand, and they explored the meadow together.

Among the fauna spotted on their hiking tour were several squirrels darting up and down trees, birds of various colors who provided an acoustic concert of sorts, and a doe, closely followed by her fawn. The sight of the mother and baby melted Wendy's heart.

"Why is it that baby animals elicit such a softening reaction in us?" Wendy marveled.

"This little guy is precioso." Karmen pulled her phone out for a video.

Wendy watched the pair of deer move through the trees and graze on the underbrush before their tour moved along.

As they approached the final stretch to the cabin, Wendy overheard Emily. "We should write a song about all this," she suggested to Michael. The two carried the discussion the rest of the way back.

"And that concludes your guided hike," Tessa said with a smile as they reached the cabin. "It's been a pleasure to be with you guys today. Do you have any questions?"

Emily and Michael approached Tessa, asking about the types of flowers and trees they'd seen. Emily pulled out her phone with pictures she'd taken, and Tessa expertly explained about the flora. Michael stood by with that soft-eyed expression he'd shown earlier.

John and Karmen were hovering over a ladybug working its way over a bush, observing the insect with intent.

Wendy regarded John and Karmen, and Michael and Emily. Her brothers were happy, and she had Evan by her side. She sighed in satisfaction.

Evan suddenly flinched next to her.

"Evan, what..." she started to ask. She turned to Evan and saw Peter standing behind him, with one of the wooden swords at Evan's back.

CHAPTER TWENTY-FIVE

Peter went to work that day intent on apologizing to Tessa. It felt like a safe place to approach her. He came in through the employee entrance at the back and asked one of the guides where she was.

The guide hesitated. "I'm not sure she'd want to see you."

Peter remembered Tessa telling him their coworkers knew how he'd treated her. They'd been protective of her ever since.

He cleared his throat. "I intend to apologize for what I did."

The man nodded. "She's out on a tour anyway. Also, it's a long story, but there's a stack of wooden swords in the storage room. The owners will probably be back to pick them up."

What an odd thing to leave at a hiking establishment. Or to even bring to a hiking establishment. Peter shrugged off the absurdity and settled himself at the front desk.

During a lull in business, Peter rose from the desk and unlocked the storage room, curious to see the forgotten swords. Sure enough, there sat the stack leaning against a corner at the back of the room. He approached them and picked one up, shocked to discover their sturdiness. He set the sword down, then locked the room up and went back to work.

An hour later, bored and tired of sitting, he stood to stretch and take a small walk. He slipped through the front door while everyone seemed occupied and entered the sunny afternoon. His body relaxed in the sunshine, and he rehearsed his apology to Tessa again in his mind, reminding himself that this was an important step to improving his life. Perhaps she'd even smile when he told her he'd set up an appointment for counseling. Yes, he was ready to speak to her and ask her forgiveness.

What he wasn't ready for was the sight of Tessa herself with her tour group when he rounded the corner of the building. He retreated, meaning to go back inside and wait till she was finished with the group.

He was fully unprepared to see that this group consisted of John, Michael, and Wendy.

Wendy, whom he also meant to apologize to. His chest clenched remembering the snake trick.

Not ready to face her yet, he stepped back and decided he'd stay in the building until she and her brothers and their group left. Then he'd approach Tessa and—

He took in the companions Wendy, John, and Michael had with them. He didn't recognize the women, but the man. That loathsome man who held Wendy's hand.

Shock struck through his chest when he saw the man's face. He knew that face. He hated that face. He felt his own face contort in anger as coherent thought fled entirely.

Hook *was* in the real world. It was impossible, but here he was. And Peter intended to do something about it.

His conscience pleaded with him to remember the reconciliation he sought.

"Reconciling be hanged," Peter fumed to himself. "He's not supposed to be here."

He whirled around and ran into the cabin. He unlocked the storage room, went straight for the stack of swords, and grabbed two of them, one in each hand. He exited through the employee door to avoid detection and slipped outside.

Anger fumed through his brain and body as he crept toward Hook. When he was within range, he nudged Hook's back with one of the swords. Hook froze but didn't turn around.

Wendy turned to address Hook, calling him Evan.

Evan?

Her face registered shock upon seeing Peter.

Peter narrowed his eyes. How could she betray him—truly betray him—and befriend his enemy?

CHAPTER TWENTY-SIX

E van didn't know what poked his back, but if Wendy's facial expression was any indication, it wasn't good. Wendy's eyes darted between Evan and whatever was behind him, her jaw agape.

"*Hook.*"

It'd been years since he'd heard that voice, but Evan instantly recognized it. Suppressed anger surfaced, heating his neck.

"Peter," Evan ground out.

He turned to Wendy and his anger dropped a few degrees. Wendy's safety was his top priority.

"Is that a *sword*?" John cried, pointing to Peter. "Where did he get a sword?"

Tessa's mouth hung open. "The ones the people left behind."

"Yes, yes, I found their swords," Peter said, irritated. "Now let's see if this *pirate* still knows how to use one."

Just as Evan wondered if a wooden sword could hurt, Peter nudged it hard into Evan's back. Yes, they could hurt.

Evan turned and simultaneously stepped away in one movement, now out of Peter's range and further from Wendy to keep her out of harm's way.

Wendy's eyes were wide. "Peter, this is madness."

"*I'm* mad?" Peter cried. "You know what's really maddening? Having a friend turn on you, taking sides with the enemy." He shot his finger out at Evan. "Romantically, even. It's not only maddening, Wendy, it's shameful. It's betrayal!" Peter fumed in anger. "How could you do this to me?"

John and Michael inched their way to Peter, their hands stretched out toward the wooden swords. But Peter's reflexes had always been quick, and he shifted position to point the other sword at them. They stopped with their hands up, then backed away and herded Emily and Karmen several yards away from the chaos.

Peter glanced at Evan. "Just like old times, eh, *Captain*?"

He flipped the sword at Evan, who caught it deftly with his left hand. Evan darted further back to keep the others out of sword-range.

Evan wasn't keen on fighting Peter. But if Peter wanted a fight, Evan could hold his own. The tricky part would be fighting without his hook—he'd never fought Peter without it. But Peter had always been able to fly during their duels, something he couldn't do here.

They circled one another, their swords out, each step filled with purpose. Evan continued to angle his steps away from the group and Peter followed.

Delivering the first strike had always been Captain Hook's habit during their skirmishes. He'd been blinded by hate for Peter, thirsty to cut him anywhere with the sword or his hook.

Memories of those hate-filled encounters surfaced, and Evan worked to channel his anger productively. Loathing radiated from Peter's face, and from what Evan remembered of their battles, Peter's strength grew with intense emotions.

Peter's steps slowed, then stopped. He bent his knees ever so slightly. Evan braced himself.

Without warning, Peter shot forward, swinging his sword vertically. Evan blocked the move, but just barely. Peter shot back again, springing forward sooner. Evan blocked the blow again.

Peter then came at Evan directly, slashing his sword this way and that. He pressed upon Evan—*thwack! tak! whoosh! thwack!*

Peter swung high, and Evan bent backward from the waist to dodge. Peter swung low, and Evan tuck jumped over Peter's weapon, making Peter growl in frustration. Evan swung low, and Peter flipped backwards in the air, agilely landing on his feet.

He then landed an especially heavy thrust, swinging his sword down and across at Evan, who defended the blow with an upswing as sweat slid down his back. They stood locked in a standstill with their swords pressed against each other. The tension strained Evan's body from head to toe.

"Why are you here?" Peter screamed in Evan's face. "You're supposed to be back in Neverland. How dare you follow me! And *how dare* you turn my friends against me." He panted, fury etched every line of his face.

"I didn't follow you." Evan's anger rose at Peter's accusations. Especially at the notion that he'd turned Wendy against Peter. Peter had done that on his own.

Peter inhaled deeply through his nose. "Yes, you did," he growled. The force of his anger thrust Evan back several paces. He stumbled and fell, throwing his right arm out to brace for impact. He landed on his elbow, pain shooting up his arm as he skidded in the dirt. Peter came at Evan again, swinging down another blow at him. Evan blocked it, but it was more luck than skill considering his position.

"Bad form!" John shouted. "*Never* attack a man when he's down. You taught us that, Peter."

Peter sobered a degree and retreated two paces, still panting. Evan caught his breath enough to jump to a standing position, blood dripping down his right arm.

Peter's breathing slowed. "Why are you here, Hook? *How* are you here?" He aimed his sword at Evan, but his body language showed no sign of imminent attack.

Evan sighed. "I stowed away on your ship."

Peter laughed humorlessly. "You? The great *Captain Hook*, stowing away on a ship? That's pathetic." He swung his sword in a circle at his side, then leveled it at Evan. "Though I suppose that answers the How. Now answer the Why—*why* are you here?"

Evan closed his eyes at Peter's insult, fighting the urge to throw slander back at this selfish being who insisted on a fight. After a breath, he opened his eyes and exhaled a portion of his anger. "I wanted a new start. I was tired of being a villain."

Peter fumed. "You're lying."

Evan scowled. "Is that so hard to believe, Peter? Haven't you ever wanted another chance?"

Peter's eyes darted to Tessa, then Wendy.

Wendy.

Evan had some choice words for Peter about Wendy. With his sword kept protectively in front of him with his left hand, he pointed his right arm toward Wendy.

"What about Wendy?"

Peter's eyebrows contracted. "What about her?"

"You've been her hero for ages, Peter—" Evan said.

"And I still am," Peter interrupted.

Evan shook his head. "Daft boy. What sort of hero subjects his friend to an incident that leaves her so terror-stricken that she faints?"

Peter seemed to struggle for words. "The snake? It was just a prank—"

"And treats her as anything less than the indescribably amazing woman she is? Flirting with other girls in front of her? Pursuing other relationships when you knew she wanted you? How is that heroic, Peter? It's undeniably bad form."

Peter's eyes darted between Wendy and Evan, his eyebrows slanted. "But I—"

"And what of the other people you've misused?" Evan continued.

Peter's eyes turned to Tessa again and his frown deepened. "Enough," he called while lowering his sword.

Evan forged on. "Everything I've worked for since arriving here has been to leave the villain behind and create a life without anger and hate. The hook is still in Neverland—physically and symbolically."

He lowered his weapon, with no intention to raise it other than to protect himself. "I'm also learning how to forgive. I've forgiven myself. I'm striving to forgive you." He took a cleansing breath as a healing energy spread through him.

Peter scoffed. "You, having need to forgive *me*?" He flipped his sword overhead and caught it without looking. "And what have you to forgive me for, Hook?"

"His name is Evan," Wendy called out.

Peter turned to the group. "Will you lot just stay out of this?"

"No," John called back.

Peter scrunched his eyes and shook his head.

⚮

Though Peter hated to admit it, what Hook said was true—Peter had been a poor excuse of a hero. He realized this in the woods recently. He came today to apologize to Tessa, attempting to right the wrongs he'd done.

Adventurous as it was to cross swords with Hook again, even wooden ones, this version of the Neverland villain lacked the rage and fervor Peter was accustomed to. This version of Hook emanated an unwillingness to injure, seeking only to defend himself from Peter's attacks.

But what revelation was this that Captain Hook could be reformed? The terror of Neverland discarding his former ways *and* his hook? Peter didn't want to believe it, yet the evidence stood before him.

An epiphany struck Peter just then. If such a treacherous being as Captain Hook could be salvaged, could the same reality be true for Peter?

His conscience refused suppression any longer. Clearly the man named Hook was no longer who he'd been. And Peter's poor choices, though seemingly justifiable before, were worth shedding to reveal a truly heroic version of himself. Peter's curiosity wondered what sort of development he might undergo through this reform, as painful as it may seem.

He'd taken risks in his lifetime—wonderful, thrilling, adventure-filled risks. But the risk before him topped them all.

His eyes scanned the group, fear and apprehension in each of their eyes. Evan's right arm had a streak of dried blood from his elbow to his wrist. This wasn't the life he wanted.

He swallowed, then threw down the wooden sword. It clattered on the ground as he inhaled deeply to say what needed to be said. "I've been selfish. And I," he shut his eyes before continuing, "I want to change."

The energy it took to say those words was more than he could manage, and he fell to his knees, his whole body deflating.

His eyes turned to Hook, or Evan, or whatever he called himself now. Evan's face registered shock. Peter turned to the group. Wendy's hands covered her mouth and nose, and tears shimmered in her eyes. John's mouth resembled a large O. Michael and their friends stood by with sober expressions.

Tessa's hands hid her mouth, and her eyebrows lifted. When she caught Peter's gaze, she dropped her hands from her face, revealing a smile. Which extremely puzzled Peter, given the way he'd hurt her.

Evan tossed his sword on the ground and approached Peter. Peter stood, unsure what to expect. He certainly didn't expect Evan's outstretched left hand.

Peter took a half-step back and eyed Evan warily. Old instinct told him not to trust this person who looked like Hook but behaved like a civilized man.

Reform. He swallowed and clasped hands with Evan.

Somewhere between his confession and the handshake, Peter felt a weight lift from his soul. Even flying hadn't been this liberating.

Chapter Twenty-seven

The group parted awkwardly from Peter. Tessa remained, which puzzled him. Hadn't she made it perfectly clear how angry she was with him? He didn't blame her though—he'd used her horribly.

But there she was, the only person remaining after Wendy and the rest of the group left. Peter was determined to apologize properly to Tessa. He stepped toward her, hefting a sword in each hand.

As he approached her, she folded her arms, and a corner of her mouth lifted.

Peter stopped and regarded her, confused. He turned around, wondering if her smile was meant for someone behind him.

He had remarkably quick reflexes, but nothing could've prepared him for the kiss on the cheek she gave him when he faced her again. He dropped both swords, which landed on each other. He stood there, his jaw dropped, while Tessa regarded him with thoughtful eyes.

"I'm proud of you." Her smile widened, enhancing her lovely features.

He felt his eyebrows shoot up in shock and his head reared back slightly. "You are?"

Tessa nodded gently. "I didn't think you'd come to terms with yourself. But I'm glad I was wrong."

Peter's relief was immediate. He felt his face break into a grin—a wholesome, altruistic, humble grin. When did Tessa's good opinion become important to him?

Tessa studied the trees before turning back to him. "Can we start over?"

"Tessa," he said. "I should be the one asking *you* for a redo."

"How about a walk? I'd love to hear how you got to this point. We're closed now, anyway." She nodded toward the building. "I'll just go clock-out."

Peter cleared his throat. "And I'll just go put these away before clocking-out," he said, nudging one of the swords with his foot.

"You've got some serious sword skills, you know," Tessa said.

Peter felt something akin to gratitude mixed with a desire to please the woman next to him.

After settling everything at the cabin, they walked through the woods while Peter recounted his inward revelations and the eagerness he felt to change. He told her of his appointment with a counselor. She directed him to online resources to further aid his mission.

There likely wouldn't be any relationship between them beyond friendship. But what a friend to have on his side. One who cared enough to assist him in the transformative journey ahead.

CHAPTER TWENTY-EIGHT

Later that summer, the former Lost Boys had called for a much-needed retreat into the mountains to escape their current occupations for a short amount of time, and Peter found this the perfect opportunity to practice the skills he'd been learning in counseling.

But he required support, and Tessa had been willing to fill such a role.

"You're gonna do great," she reassured him as he drove with her to the meeting spot in the mountains. "You've made a lot of progress in a short time. Things will get better with your friends."

Peter drew in a breath and released it slowly. "What if I forget everything and react?"

"Worst case scenario—you come away knowing more about what you can work on in the future."

Peter couldn't help but reach for Tessa's hand, which rested on the console between them. A gesture of gratitude rather than romance. She squeezed his hand as they pulled into the dirt parking area near the meeting spot.

They followed the trail leading to a healthy campfire surrounded by laughter and conversation. Thomas, Slater, Coby, and Nick sat next to each other on a fallen log. John and Karmen sat close to each other on a wide tree stump. And Michael huddled next to Emily, whispering something that made her laugh. Some of the group roasted hot dogs, but most were roasting marshmallows.

Peter introduced Tessa to the Boys before picking up marshmallow roasting equipment. Then Thomas gave an unsolicited monologue on the proper way to roast a marshmallow.

After two minutes of Thomas's soliloquy, Peter wanted to tune him out or spout a snarky comment as he would have before.

He turned to Tessa for some encouragement. She sat with a glazed-over expression, blinking every ten seconds, and Peter pinched his lips closed to keep a laugh inside. Even she was losing interest in Thomas's long-winded explanation. She startled and yelped when her marshmallow caught on fire.

Peter took the roasting stick from her hands and blew out the flame. He pulled the charred goo off the stick with a napkin and replaced it with a fresh mallow. Then he flipped the stick in the air and caught it while holding Tessa's gaze. Her mouth parted and her eyes went wide. They also glanced at his mouth, sending a thrill through his sternum.

"Thank you," she said while retrieving the roasting stick from his outstretched hand.

He glanced briefly at her lips, then nodded, reminding himself they were merely friends. She was only there for support.

Several weeks of counseling proved beneficial in helping Peter work through his issues. The progress came steadily, though not overnight. But at this point, deliberately doing things to help others, such as assisting Tessa with her burned mallow, began to bring him a kind of happiness he hadn't known before. He wished he'd started it sooner.

Peter returned his attention to Thomas, who rotated a mallow over the fire. Peter caught the key movements, then reached out to help Tessa do likewise.

Thomas finally (mercifully) ended his speech and stuffed the toasted confection into his mouth. "Is that your fourth s'more, Coby?" he asked after swallowing.

Coby nodded as bits of crumbs outlined his mouth.

Thomas's mouth contorted in confusion. "How is it you can eat like that and still maintain all that muscle? It goes against nature. Eating sweets and junk ought to have you looking flabby and soft, like me. Except I'm conscious of my sugar intake—I limit it whenever possible." He then pulled his second toasted mallow from his stick and stuffed it in his mouth.

Michael quietly snort-laughed from across the circle.

"What?" Thomas demanded, mouth full of mallow goo.

"Do you remember what Coby does for a living?" Michael asked while gesturing to the man in question.

Thomas's face screwed up in thought.

Coby answered after swallowing the last of his s'more. "I move heavy stuff around all day, remember?"

Thomas showed no signs of recognition. He merely blinked slowly while chewing the mallow.

Peter's irritation surfaced at Thomas's ignorance. Tessa must've sensed his agitation since her hand moved gently to his leg—a reminder to practice patience.

Peter relaxed at the gesture. "He works for a moving company, Thomas," he said. "He essentially exercises all day. He can afford to eat like that and still maintain his physique."

Tessa lightly squeezed her hand on Peter's thigh, a gesture of congratulations.

Coby lifted his fifth s'more in salute to Peter with a grin on his face.

"Though truly," Slater piped up. "You ought to draw the line somewhere with all those s'mores."

Coby shrugged and nodded. "I can stop. I don't want cavities, anyway."

Thomas suddenly surveyed the group. "Is Wendy joining us this evening? I ought to have worn something nicer." He dusted off his khaki pants, incidentally smearing dirt and mallow residue from his hands.

Michael cleared his throat. "No, she's out with her boyfriend tonight."

The declaration stung Peter for an infinitesimal moment before he reminded himself that Wendy was never his to begin with, and he'd given her very little reason to trust him in the past. He closed his eyes and pictured future times where he would treat her with every bit of respect she deserved. He nodded to himself, one corner of his mouth lifting.

Thomas' excitement dimmed. "Oh," he said, his voice low. "She's dating someone, then?"

Michael nodded.

Thomas sighed. "Well, I always knew she was too good for me, anyway." He straightened and put his roasting stick down, then his face brightened. "But there's a girl who often studies at the law library when I'm there. I've caught her sending smiles my way several times. I believe she's quite taken with me."

Nick and Slater snickered from their seats next to Peter. He nudged them, trying to hide his own amused smile.

"What?" Thomas asked. "I'm in law school. I'm quite the catch."

Slater rolled his eyes before turning to Michael. "Who is Wendy dating? Is he a good match for her?"

"Emily has a few pictures of them," Michael supplied.

She pulled her phone out and handed it to Slater. "Aren't they cute together?" she said.

Slater, Nick, and Thomas crouched around Emily's phone. With each picture they scrolled through, their eyes grew wider.

After perhaps the fifth picture, Nick gasped. "Isn't that *him*?"

"Him who?" Emily asked with slanted brows.

"Evan resembles someone we all know from before we moved here," Michael explained.

Slater pointed at Emily's phone. "No, that's got to be *him*. His right hand is missing—it's Hook."

Karmen tsked. "Just because he's missing a hand doesn't mean you gotta be snarky about it."

Peter couldn't contain the laugh that surfaced, breaking free and echoing in the trees surrounding them. A laugh free from conceit, judgement, or mockery. A pure laugh that diffused the tension and fear that had thickened among Slater, Nick, and Thomas.

The group was suddenly laughing with Peter, and his soul expanded as he shared equality with his peers rather than demanding their admiration.

Chapter Twenty-nine

Summer faded to fall, with shades of red, orange, and yellow creeping down the mountain foliage to the metropolitan area.

And into the pediatric clinic where Wendy and Karmen worked. They stayed after hours one night to set up fall and Halloween decorations.

Wendy stood on a chair to reach the higher areas of the wall to tape decorative leaves and black bats on.

She saw Karmen turn from draping a leaf-strewn garland across the ceiling.

"Chica, you are too short to reach that spot and you're gonna break your neck," Karmen called from across the room.

Wendy inched her fingers upward to stick a leaf on a selected spot. "I'm fine. See?" She succeeded, but she heard Karmen's determined footsteps approach.

"What would Evan do if you fell and died? And how could I face John if I let his sister do something like that and get hurt? No." She took the decorations from Wendy's hands. "You're getting down right now and putting these on that wall over there." She pointed to the toddler area, surrounded by a half-wall.

Wendy huffed and snatched the decorations back before marching over to cover the assigned area. She soon heard Karmen climb onto the same chair she'd just been evicted from and turned to see her decorating the high wall behind the front desk.

"Karmen," Wendy laughed. "You sneaky hypocrite."

"I'm like four inches taller than you. Go back to decorating the pony wall while I put this garland up here."

Once they'd finished their work, they stood back and admired the fall-filled waiting room.

"I think this looks better than last year," Wendy said.

"That's because you and I did it this year and not the office staff. They're all as short as you, but less creative." Karmen gave Wendy a side glance while smirking.

"Simply because I'm not as tall as you doesn't mean I'm vertically challenged. And Evan doesn't mind my height." Wendy smiled as she thought of how her head fit well into the curve between Evan's chin and neck.

"Hola? Are you gone already?" Karmen waved her hand in front of Wendy's face.

She swatted it away as they both giggled. "John doesn't seem to mind you being near his height."

"It's true. I think he likes my long legs." Karmen winked.

"New subject matter."

"No, John is a great subject matter. He treats me like a goddess."

Wendy shook her head. "I never imagined him being cognizant of the world around him enough to notice women in general, let alone be in a relationship with one."

"I made sure I got his attention. Now if only I could get him to kiss me."

"He hasn't? Never mind. We truly need a new topic."

"I know," Karmen conceded with a sly smile. "Let's talk about you and Evan."

Wendy put away the decorating supplies. "Let's do."

"How long have you guys been dating now?"

Wendy paused to calculate the time. "Five months. And I've loved it."

"You've *loved* it, hm?" Karmen nudged as they headed to the nurse's station to gather their things. "As in, you enjoy it lots, or you're in love with him already?"

Wendy could tell Karmen was teasing, but the question struck Wendy. She paused as she picked up her bag and jacket.

She *did* love him. How long had she loved him? The memory of him in his captain's uniform with his hair waving in the wind on the deck of his ship shot thrills through her body.

Then he'd shown up in her life again, a reformed version of the sexy pirate captain. And of all the miracles, he wanted her. He held her in his arms every chance he could and kissed her into blissful oblivion.

Karmen broke Wendy from her revelation. "You've got it bad, amiga."

"I can't deny it. You've got quite the observation skills, Karmen."

"It's what balances me and John. He's clueless, and I miss nothing." She slipped her bag over her shoulder and the two friends giggled as they left the clinic.

CHAPTER THIRTY

What could be more fitting in autumn than a pumpkin spice pastry? But pumpkin spice goodness wasn't why Peter was determined to be on time for his meeting with Wendy. Punctuality showed respect, and if anyone deserved respect, she did.

He rushed into the bakery and took stock of all the tables. Wendy's absence confirmed he'd arrived early.

He slowed his steps and made his way to an empty table. Though his gait could no longer be called a swagger, his strides still held self-assurance.

He pondered the shift his life had taken. He was still intelligent, agile, and as fiercely good-looking as ever, if he were being honest. He tried not to let it go to his head though. And he stopped flirting with and ogling every woman that walked past.

He checked his phone for the time, then glanced up as Wendy arrived. He waved his hand to catch her attention, and a small smile formed on her mouth.

A smile was a good sign since he had a heavy apology to administer.

He stood to greet her and pulled her chair out.

"Such good manners," Wendy said, sounding surprised as she sat down.

Peter feigned incredulity with his hand on his chest. "Has it ever been otherwise?"

Her eyebrow lifted, immediately humbling him and setting his apology into motion. "Wendy, I've been a daft, self-seeking imbecile since we met. I meant what I said when I told everyone I wanted to change."

"How's that coming along?" Wendy leaned her elbows on the table.

"Fantastically. I've been with the counselor for months. The world is a new place for me with my eyes opened to my mistakes. I even spent an evening with the Lost Boys without lashing out or mocking them."

"That *is* progress," Wendy conceded. "What are your goals going forward?"

"My top priority today is apologizing to you. And to confess something awful I did. Do you remember the snake on your doorstep?"

Wendy inhaled and let it out slowly. "I wondered if that was you."

Peter's eyes went wide as mild panic set in. "You did? I'm so sorry—I should never have done that to you. It was incredibly foolish. It was a misguided attempt to prove a point and make you see me as your hero again. But no explanation can justify what I did. I knew snakes terrified you, and I waited until you were near fainting before stepping in. It wasn't even a rattlesnake."

"Was it a gopher snake?"

"Yes," Peter said with surprise. "How did you know?"

"Long story." She swallowed. "I truly was terrified, Peter. Even more so than any encounter with the croc."

"What I did was inexcusable." He reached out and touched her arm. "I hope you can forgive me."

Wendy nodded. "I can forgive you, but it'll take time to trust you again."

"I'll do all I can to earn your trust. Please say we can still be friends."

Her lips spread into a smile. "I think we can do that."

A waitress approached at that moment carrying a large white pastry box tied with orange ribbon. She set it in front of Wendy and left.

Wendy's curiosity filled her face. "What's this?"

"A peace offering of sorts. It's a bit of every fall flavored pastry from the bakery. Pumpkin bread, apple cider donuts, pumpkin chocolate cookies, apple cinnamon muffins, and a few others I can't recall right now. I hope you like them."

Wendy smirked. "You can't buy my trust, you know."

Peter chuckled. "I know. This comes with no strings attached and no expectations. Just a gift from one friend to another. You can share them or eat every last crumb on your own." He winked before pushing his chair back. "But now, I must leave. Thank you for meeting with me. It means more than you know."

Which it truly did. Wendy would've had every right to refuse to see him, and she could have shut down his apology and denied his wish for friendship. But she'd come, and she'd welcomed the plea for friendship.

A lump settled in Peter's throat, and he willed the tears stinging his eyes to stay put until he let them flow freely in his car.

He felt in his soul that circumstances would continue to improve, and if he could still fly through happy thoughts, he could've soared the Earth's entire perimeter.

CHAPTER THIRTY-ONE

What would October be without an ample amount of candy corn?

Evan would've called that an improvement.

"How can you eat that? It's nothing but sugared wax." He gestured to Michael and John, who shared a dish of the questionable candy.

Wendy and Evan sat with John, Karmen, Michael, and Emily in the Darlings' townhome one night in early October, the candy corn being passed around.

"Are you kidding?" Karmen said with wide eyes. "It's not Halloween without candy corn." She scooped a handful and poured it into her mouth.

"Amen to that," John agreed as he picked up a few more for himself.

"Isn't it a strange holiday, though?" Michael piped in. "Dressing up as anything you wish and indulging in a gluttonous amount of sugar, all in the name of a fall festival?"

"Bring it on," Emily said from beside him while chewing. She finished and swallowed. "What're you guys gonna be for Halloween?"

"Aren't we all a bit old to be dressing up?" John said. "I mean, it's a children's holiday, isn't it?"

Karmen gasped, causing John to startle. "I almost forgot! The clinic is throwing a Halloween party, and the pediatricians go all-out. We need to get costumes."

Evan pursed his lips and considered the idea. It didn't sound too terrible. "As long as they don't serve candy corn."

Wendy nudged him with her knee. "Even if they do, no one will force you to eat it."

Emily clapped her hands. "This is gonna be so fun. What should our costumes be?"

She'd turned to face Michael, who sat with a comically shocked expression. "*Our* costumes?"

"Yeah, if we're going together let's do something coordinated. You know, like a famous couple." She suddenly blushed. "Or, I mean, we don't have to do a couple's thing. We could be something like peanut butter and jelly."

Michael took her hand and caught her attention. "I think a couple's theme is a grand idea."

Emily's smile broke through her embarrassment and suddenly the matter was settled.

Wendy leaned in to whisper to Evan, "The more they spend time together, the less I believe their claim as 'just friends'."

Evan leaned in to whisper back, "I'll be curious to see what costume idea they decide on. Do you have any ideas for us?" He tilted his head and nuzzled his nose into her neck.

Wendy melted into him. "I think I have a few we could work with."

"Hey! No kissing in here," John protested.

Evan and Wendy sighed simultaneously while moving apart, and Evan fought back the laugh that threatened to break free at the sight of Karmen's longing expression toward John. The man clearly needed to wake up and kiss her before she went mad.

"Tell me about your ideas, then," Evan prompted from a John-approved distance.

"Alright," Wendy began. "Hear me out ..."

"You're going as what?" Coby asked from the driver's seat of the moving van.

"You heard me right," Evan said then sighed. "Phantom of the Opera. She saw the musical on stage, then we watched the movie together one night. It was the only one of her ideas I could agree to and still keep my dignity."

Coby chuckled. "Now I'm curious. What were her other ideas?" Evan groaned, but Coby persisted. "They can't be *that* bad."

"A pair of zombie lovers. A mermaid and a sailor. Or ..." He cleared his throat. "Tinkerbell and Peter Pan."

Coby laughed. "Was she kidding? Like they'd ever be a couple."

"Especially since she didn't make it here to Reality. I think Wendy was only half-joking. But yes, the Phantom was my best option. She said she couldn't wait to see me with the mask."

Coby continued to snicker as he navigated through the streets to their customer's house. "Who else is going?"

"John and Karmen, and Michael and Emily. I believe you met the girls this summer." Coby nodded before Evan continued. "However, Emily expressed some reserve about going, since her older sister also wants to attend but doesn't have a date. Not that she needs a date to attend, but since Emily is going with Michael..."

"The sister probably doesn't want to be left out. Hm." Coby became silent for a few moments before offering, "I could go with her sister."

Evan's lips pursed. "You'd do a blind date?"

"Sure. I'm always down for making new friends. Have Emily give her my number." A pause. "What's her name?"

"Alexis. You're certain you wouldn't mind?"

"Yeah, I'm sure. It'll be fun."

Evan texted Wendy about the latest development, asking her opinion on the matter. Not that he needed her permission, he simply valued her input.

He valued everything about her. How would it be to see her every day but not have to bid her goodbye at the end of it? What would a life together be like? He'd found her again, and he had no intention of letting her go. A future with her unfolded before him in his mind. A future with a home and family. Children. Pets? Did Wendy want pets? She'd had a dog growing up in London ...

"Evan," Coby drew out his name. "You still with me, bro? You look like you're panicking."

Evan blinked several times before remembering where he was and what he was doing. "Are we almost there?"

Coby huffed a laugh. "You are *so* thinking about Wendy, aren't you?"

Evan smiled and glanced at Coby. "Maybe ..."

"Okay, but what's with your facial expression? I've seen you distracted thinking about her, but never, like, *nervous* distracted. You guys okay?"

"Of course," he said, casting a brief smile in Coby's direction.

Coby shook his head as he parked at their destination. "I'm still in the dark here, Evan. Help me out."

Evan inhaled a breath and let it out slowly to calm his anxiousness. "I love Wendy."

"And ...?" Coby asked with an expectant look.

"You don't sound surprised."

"It's pretty obvious how you feel about her."

"Oh. Well, I want her in my life."

"She *is* in your life, bro."

"No, I mean, I want her in my future as well as my present. I want to ask her to marry me."

Coby's jaw dropped, his eyes widening at the same time. "That's awesome!" He pulled Evan into a Coby-size hug. "Congrats!"

"Thank you," Evan wheezed.

"Sorry." Coby released Evan from the stronghold. "But, like, not sorry at the same time. I'm so excited for you!"

Evan laughed shakily and shook his head. "I haven't asked her yet. I want to ask her soon, but I'm not sure how."

"I'm pretty sure it's a simple question."

"I want to do something unique—something worth remembering."

"I love happily ever afters," Coby squeaked as tears formed in his eyes. "What kind of unique thing are you thinking of?"

"You know the Halloween party we were talking about?"

CHAPTER THIRTY-TWO

Peter opened the passenger door for Tessa after they celebrated his progress in therapy with milkshakes.

"Thanks," she said while slipping out of the car.

"Thank *you* for helping me get to this point." Peter's strides of improvement impressed even his counselor. "I wouldn't be here without you."

Tessa's head tilted to meet his eyes. "You're welcome, then." Her lips parted while her eyes searched his. "I need to tell you something."

"Tell me," he whispered, hoping it had something to do with getting back together.

"I'm moving to Washington state."

"Oh." Peter blinked, unsure what to say.

"I'm going to study environmental science at the University of Washington. I got a scholarship, and they're one of the best schools for the degree."

"Then, congratulations. That's wonderful." Except it wasn't. A piece of Peter's soul broke with the news. Tessa had become an anchor in his life. What would he do without her support?

"You'll be okay," she said as though reading his thoughts.

"Will I?" he asked with tilted brows.

"Have you thought about more school? I know you want to run your own outdoor business someday. You've got all the knowledge and skills. You just need a degree to get your own thing running."

The thought of further education had always seemed unpalatable to him. But perhaps he could picture himself studying business and establishing his own company, taking clients out year-round on hiking treks. He'd be his own boss and do what he loved to do.

Tessa called his attention back. "Sorry I kinda sprung that on you. I didn't know if I'd get in, and I didn't want to say anything until I knew."

Peter blinked several times, forcing himself to accept her news. "I'm happy for you."

Tessa swallowed. "Thanks for letting me be part of your life."

"Thank you for improving it." His heart was suddenly in his throat. "When do you leave?"

"The semester doesn't start till January, but I want a few months to get settled first and find a job before school starts. I'll be going next week."

Peter's mouth opened and closed. "Is this goodbye, then?"

She nodded. "Probably."

"Can I give you something before you go? Wendy once called it a thimble."

Her eyes darted to his lips and her breath came out in a shudder. "Yes."

Peter moved his hand gently behind her neck as her eyes fluttered shut. With her lack of protest, he moved forward. She tilted her head up and slid her hands to his waist. Then Peter leaned down and pressed his lips to hers. Her hands tightened on his shirt, and she led the kiss forward. Moments later they parted, heads leaning on each other. Peter felt her tears fall on his arms. He tilted her chin up with his knuckles, kissed her gently on the lips, and wiped her tears with his thumb.

"You'll do wondrous things, Tessa," he whispered. "Wondrous things."

She smiled through her tear-streaked face. "Promise me you won't break too many hearts, Peter," she teased.

"I promise."

Tessa walked away to her apartment, leaving an ache in Peter's soul. She'd been the catalyst to his transformative journey, and she'd been with him during each phase of change.

You'll be okay, she'd said.

He'd come this far, and he could go further still. Surely life had more adventures in store.

The tightness in his throat became swallowed up in his determination to make his life the best it could be.

Chapter Thirty-three

In Wendy's opinion, there are Halloween decorations, and then there are *tasteful* Halloween decorations. The type that transfers you to a new place, a new time, and causes you to forget the here-and-now with all its whimsy.

These were her thoughts as she and Evan entered the Halloween party. Faux sconces and chandeliers lined and topped the room. Richly colored fabric draped the walls, and flickering candles lined refreshment tables and sitting areas. Large, painted pictures of personages long gone hung on the walls, draped in spider webs. The old vogue gave a haunting flair to the decor that left nothing to be wanted.

"Our attire matches the time period in here," Evan observed as they entered the breathtaking scene.

The low lighting gave Evan an even sexier hue than his already tempting costume. Wendy's heart sped in her throat, and she imagined her and Evan in that era living out the scene around them. They'd sneak around a corner somewhere down a dimly lit hallway, and he'd pull her into his arms ...

"Where are your thoughts, Miss Darling?" Evan asked with a knowing smirk. "Are you salivating from hunger, thirst, or something else?"

Truly she'd love to drink in Evan from masked face to booted feet. They should remember to rent these costumes next year.

"I think you know well enough where my thoughts are," she answered while sliding her hand over his lapel. His black tuxedo was the shade of his dark hair, and the white mask made a stark contrast. His forget-me-not eyes stood out fiercely from his black and white ensemble.

Wendy's cream-colored lacy gown draped down to floor-length, the neckline sitting just off her shoulders. She'd done her hair in a mass of curls and set it in a half-up hairstyle. Yes, she'd remember to get these costumes again next year.

Where would she and Evan be a year from now? She set aside the topic and focused on the present while craning her head to search the crowd. "Do you see John or Michael yet?"

Evan nodded toward the entrance on the opposite side of the room. "There's Michael and Emily over there." He raised his hand to catch their attention, and the teenagers trotted over to join them.

Emily gasped. "The Phantom and Christine Daaé! I love it." She touched Wendy's gown, commenting on the lace and fawning over her curly hair. "My hair won't curl like that—it only knows how to go straight."

Emily's hair was also pulled half-up. It showed off her shoulders nicely, as did the white sleeveless dress and angel wings she wore.

"I say straight hair is just the thing," Michael said next to Emily. He wore a fabric silver knight's uniform, his head uncovered.

Emily turned to Michael with a gentle smile and slipped her hand into his.

"These are lovely costumes," Wendy said. "What are you supposed to be?"

Emily smoothed her white dress with her free hand. "We're Romeo and Juliet from the 90s movie. I made Michael watch it with me once, and we thought it'd be a fun costume. There's John and Karmen."

Wendy turned and her eyes widened. "What a pair you two are."

A pair of Flamenco dancers, to be precise. Karmen's red dress, adorned with black lace, hugged her body down to her knees, where it flared in a layer of ruffles. Large silk roses topped her dark hair, which was pulled back in a bun.

John's dark hair complimented the white shirt, black vest, black pants, and red sash of his costume.

Karmen pulled out a black lace fan, and the two of them struck a pose that would've been impressive if John could indeed strike a pose. Admittedly, he could not. However, in Wendy's opinion, Karmen's finesse made up for his lack.

The group clapped, and Karmen gushed over everyone's costumes. "You all look fantastic. Let's go get some pictures before we party."

They took turns passing around each other's phones and snapping photos.

When they finished, Emily scanned the crowd. "Alexis should be here soon."

"What costumes are she and Coby wearing?" Wendy asked.

Emily shrugged. "She said it was a surprise. But I saw a pixie costume on her bed earlier."

Karmen's eyes scanned the partygoers. "Is that Alexis over there?" She pointed to a girl in a costume that looked uncannily like Tinkerbell.

Emily nodded. "Sure is."

At that moment Coby approached Alexis, wearing what could only be the equivalent of Peter's Neverland attire. They'd dressed as Peter Pan and Tinkerbell.

Michael snickered, Evan smirked, and Wendy nudged both of them.

The two new friends stood with heads together, engrossed in some engaging conversation.

John raised his brows. "They seem cozy with each other."

"What do you think they're talking about?" Michael asked.

"I dunno, but let's go join them. Oh." Emily stopped short as Coby took Alexis's hand and pulled her to the dance floor.

"I guess we won't be joining them after all," Michael said.

Karmen sighed wistfully. "They'd make a cute couple. Isn't that sweet, John?" Her face spoke volumes of hints, but Wendy could tell John still wasn't getting it.

"Shall we get more candy corn?" he asked.

Karmen frowned. "Some people have a sense of romance and a bit of imagination." She strutted away toward the candy corn, the hem of her Flamenco dress dragging across the floor with nearly as much forlornness as her demeanor.

John blinked and turned to Wendy. "Have I missed something?"

Evan offered the advice Wendy was too reticent to share. "Romance and imagination, my friend. Have you ever *imagined* being *romantic* with Karmen?" He raised his eyebrows meaningfully.

John pursed his lips. "I'll give that some thought."

"Please do," Evan answered with a nod. He turned to Wendy and whispered, "Does he need a push? A man-to-man talk? I've never seen a woman have to give so many hints as Karmen has."

"She *is* working with John," Wendy whispered back. "But he's an intelligent man in his own way. He'll either get the hint, or she'll take control and spell the situation out for him."

Karmen returned from the candy corn table, her face set in determination.

"Hey, John," Karmen said while taking his hand. "Let's go for a walk."

"But the party's in here," he countered with confusion.

"True. But maybe we could take the party outside," Karmen said as she kissed his cheek.

Wendy noticed Evan raise his brows at John and flick his head toward the exit.

John's eyes lit with understanding, and he smiled from ear to ear as he cleared his throat.

"I think," he said to the group, "that Karmen and I will take this *party* outside." He waggled his eyebrows exaggeratedly and tugged Karmen toward the exit.

"Finalmente," Wendy heard Karmen whisper loudly as she and John made their exit.

Michael snort-laughed. "Not one for subtlety, is he?" Emily playfully swatted Michael's chest. "What?"

~

The tiny box in Evan's jacket pocket seemed to weigh as much as a cannon ball against his chest. When the ideal moment arose tonight, he'd pull out the tiny box and ask the life-altering question.

For now, he savored the warmth of Wendy's waist in his arms as they danced. She radiated everything lovely and good. And alluring, if one took into account her costume with its off-the-shoulder and low-cut bodice. Her entire attention centered on him, and in that moment the tiny box in his jacket seemed to scream.

He leaned close to her ear. "Come with me," he whispered.

One corner of her lips lifted. She moved her hand into his and they trotted through the crowded dancing area, out the exit, and into the chilly night. Light from the full moon illuminated the otherwise dark evening, casting an unearthly glow about them and enhancing the surreal moment.

Wendy pulled him with her around the corner, then pressed him flush with the building before rising on her toes and covering his mouth with hers. His arms wound around her and tightened as the intensity of her kiss increased. He wanted this so incredibly much. Oh, how he needed her.

"I love you," she breathed out.

Evan pulled back, unprepared for her declaration to come before his.

She bit her lower lip while smiling. "Evan, how could the universe bring us together again and we not take advantage of it?"

"Are you speaking to me or to my persona?" He gestured to the mask and his tuxedo while winking.

Wendy pulled the mask off and took his face in her hands. "Evander Roberts, I need you. Please say you need me too."

If ever there had been a sign given to a man to propose to a woman, this was it. And Evan would be an imbecile to disregard such an opportunity.

Evan took Wendy's left hand and kissed the inside of her wrist before lowering himself to one knee.

"I need you as well. I want you with me always." He inhaled shakily before breathing out, "And I love you."

Wendy's lips parted before spreading into a smile. Evan let go of her hand to reach into his jacket pocket, pulling out the tiny box.

Her eyes widened before shimmering tears came spilling down her face.

Evan opened the box and held it toward her, showing her a gold band topped with a single diamond. "I love you with everything I am. I cannot imagine any sort of agreeable future where you aren't in it with me. Will you have me?"

Wendy was already nodding before he finished, and Evan realized that until that moment he'd never been whole. Even with his life turned completely around, he was incomplete without her.

He rose swiftly from his knees and kissed her soundly. Their bubble was broken by the sound of applause and cheering, and they turned to see their audience. John, Karmen, Michael, and Emily positively beamed in their direction.

Wendy's hand covered her smile, and Evan pulled her closer to his side. Realizing the tiny box still held its contents, he turned to Wendy and slipped the ring onto her left hand. Then he resumed expressing his love for her through his kiss.

Epilogue

How long does it take to plan a wedding? Some insist upon more than a year or two. Others skip straight to the ceremony and elope. (This was Peter's advice to Wendy—travel to Las Vegas and have it all done quickly. His exact words were, "Why wait? Just go and make it official. Then you can honeymoon there right after.")

Wendy and Evan formulated a wonderful blend of those scenarios. Having become engaged in October, they set their wedding date for the following May.

Trusting Karmen's forthright manner, Wendy had brought her along in her search for a wedding dress. True enough, Karmen told Wendy when a dress was too long or too short, too many sequins or not enough lace, too this or too that.

Then Wendy came out in a white dress with lace sleeves that extended to her wrists and a wide neckline that accentuated her delicate collarbone. The corset bodice hugged her waist, with laces tying down the back, and the skirt flowed down to the floor in layered waves, alternating between lace and satin fabric.

At the sight of this one, Karmen simply smiled with tears in her eyes. "Perfecto."

"Though it isn't quite fair," Wendy observed as Karmen styled her hair on the day of the wedding. "Evan had such an easy experience choosing a tuxedo. He went into one store and was finished within thirty minutes."

"But we had more fun," Karmen teased as she pinned a tiny set of white roses into Wendy's updo. "And you look much better than he will."

Karmen rescinded her words when they saw Evan through the crack in the door at the back of the chapel. "Never mind. Your husband-to-be looks even better in this than in his Phantom costume."

Wendy didn't think that was possible, but Karmen's words proved true as the chapel doors opened for her to enter and the wedding music began.

John took her arm and walked her down the aisle as tears fell down his face. "I'm so happy for you both," he whispered before kissing her cheek, placing her hand in Evan's, and sitting down next to Karmen on the front row.

The ceremony was simple and sweet. Wendy and Evan had eyes only for each other, saying yes when prompted and repeating the words the pastor instructed. Rings were exchanged, they were pronounced husband and wife, and Evan was permitted to kiss the bride. Which he did with perfection.

Cheers echoed off the church walls and Wendy's heart pounded wildly. She was a married woman to a reformed man, and a beautiful future lay before them.

While neither of them could've predicted a future together, it was mutually agreed that neither of them could picture anything else but being together.

As for Happily Ever After, Wendy's life, along with her brothers and her Neverland friends, wasn't perfect. Just as life isn't perfect for anyone. But she chose happiness, and so she and Evan lived happily.

The End

A GAME OF HIDE AND SEEK

BONUS SHORT STORY

*F*ive years later

The hair on the back of Peter's neck bristled as he stood in his cabin. That sensation hadn't happened since Neverland, where he'd been stalked by Hook and his pirates, and even by Tinkerbell on occasion. The memory of those adventures surfaced, and apprehension coursed through his mind.

But those days were gone—who would stalk him in this world?

Perhaps a cougar from deep in the mountains had ventured lower. That often happened during the summer when deer herds migrated to the valley. But it was the middle of winter.

He brushed the thoughts aside while packing up his things from his stay at his cabin/office. He usually stayed a day or two after taking clients on his mountain treks.

He'd been fortunate to take the former Lost Boys and John and Michael Darling on occasion. A manly outdoor camping trip in the snow with the old group was always time well spent.

All his clients loved his guided year-round mountain adventure. Except the most recent one, which held his first and only mishap when a client ventured away from the group against Peter's rules. The client, a man named Darrell, was missing for nearly twenty-four hours in the woods, necessitating a search-and-rescue, and landing Peter with a horrible online review.

An uneasy sensation floated through his brain, and though he was certain he was alone at his cabin, his senses told him otherwise.

He made a secure search of his refurbished cabin. He'd found the run-down structure after graduating with a business degree a few years ago. His fix-it skills, curiosity, and sense of adventure proved useful as he turned the cabin from a dilapidated forgotten stack of wood into an inviting structure to situate his mountain trekking business. And given his expertise with the outdoors, the business quickly transformed into the profitable career it was at present. It also served as an affordable vacation rental from time to time.

All three bedrooms and both gathering areas appeared well enough—nothing seemed amiss. Before leaving the cabin to head to his truck, he paused at the floor-to-ceiling window overlooking a snow-covered meadow to the east.

This was living. This was liberation. Earning money doing what he loved best. Living near friends who felt like family.

A faint clang came from outside the window, breaking Peter from his musings. His eyes scanned the outdoor view left and right, but he couldn't make out anything that had made the sound. He set his mouth in a firm line as he moved from the window, retrieved his backpack, and left the cabin, locking the front door behind him.

He jogged through the snow-plowed driveway to his truck and swung the backpack in the passenger seat. He'd need freedom of movement to inspect the outdoor sound that sent the hairs on his neck on end again. Then he entered the foot-deep snow to inspect the perimeter of the cabin.

He came nearly full circle before he found the source of the noise—his pile of wood lay overturned and his barrel of ice melt was tipped on its side, the contents trailing down the hill. A set of footprints confirmed that it was vandalism. As he suspected.

Was the perpetrator still there? The uneasiness in his mind dissolved, yet the raised hair on his neck remained. Were the two sensations connected?

He searched the road—no cars, though he spotted a set of tire tracks embedded in the snowy road. He searched the surrounding trees, which hardly hid anything in their barren state. Nothing. A slog of snow rolled off the roof and landed in a heap nearby, but that was bound to happen in the winter.

Deciding some overturned supplies and some sliding snow were nothing to worry about, he climbed inside his truck, warmed the engine, and turned on alternative music before heading down the mountain to his condo in the city.

~~~

Despite checking the locks on his front door and windows, Peter still couldn't shake the hair-raising sensation, though he was now minus the apprehension.

He ordered takeout for dinner, then fell asleep to the drone of evening television on his large flat screen.

He awoke when his brain registered the absence of the TV sound. He blinked in the darkness.

Shuffling noises to his right had his senses on alert. Shifting into action, he inched his body into a crouched position on the floor in front of the couch. His ears picked up more movement from the right, closer this time. When he sensed the source of sound was close enough to tackle, he sprung toward it, knocking over a petite figure.

The figure struggled, arms and legs flipping Peter onto his back before pinning him to the ground. He went limp to feign defeat long enough for the person to relax their hold on his limbs.

Then Peter swung out with his right arm and flipped the person over, so he was now pinning *them* to the ground.

The perpetrator gave a frustrated groan. A groan he knew so well but should've been impossible in Reality. He'd left her behind in Neverland.

"Who are you?" he demanded.

A trilling laugh came before the person spoke. "Did you miss me, Peter?"

Peter's heart leaped to his throat as he exhaled an unbelieving breath. "Tink?"

～

Tink's heart pounded from the exertion and her current position with Peter's body pinning hers to the ground.

"Isn't this cozy?" she breathed.

Peter cleared his throat before standing up. Light filled the room as he flipped on the kitchen lights. "You're human size?"

Tink sat up, leaning on her elbows and scowling. "You left me."

Peter ran a hand through his hair, a gesture that had always made Tink wish she could thread her fingers through it. "How did you find me?"

How dare he avoid the topic? "You *left* me, Peter."

He opened his mouth to speak, but all he said was, "I'm sorry," and shrugged.

"You said you'd wait till the Fae Festival was over, then we'd go to Reality with the others. Your words were, 'I won't leave you behind, Tink.'" She stood and approached him. "But that's exactly what you did."

Peter turned his eyes away from hers.

"Why?" Tink demanded, fighting to stay angry even though his nearness set her nerves buzzing pleasantly.

Peter shook his head.

Tink gripped his shirt, pulling him away from the counter he leaned against. "WHY?" Tears welled in her eyes.

He finally met her stare. "I was immature, and I didn't want you to come. I thought you'd spoil the fun."

Tink's head reared back, and she shoved him against the counter. He stumbled but caught his balance before he could fall. He didn't retaliate, an uncharacteristic response for him. Or at least the boy he'd been in Neverland.

But this wasn't a boy standing before her. She'd trailed him from a distance since finding him, but she'd failed to notice one very important thing. He was a man now.

Tink's brows came together as curiosity distracted her from her anger. "You grew up."

"I did." He shrugged. "All of us did after coming here."

Tink tilted her head. "But shouldn't you be an old man by now?"

Peter shook his head, smiling. "I wouldn't be that old. Everyone else is somewhere between twenty-five and thirty by appearance."

She allowed her eyes to peruse him from his feet, up his lean torso, to his chiseled jaw. He towered over her petite form, and her pulse sped up. "You grew up nicely." She studied his eyes—they were the same shade of green as before. Those eyes that had her entranced in Neverland held the same pull here.

A corner of Peter's mouth twitched up. "Thanks."

She scowled, putting her hands on her hips. "It wasn't a compliment. Just an observation." She stepped away before turning back to him. "You said everyone else aged as well?"

Peter folded his arms and nodded. "The Lost Boys, the Darling brothers, Wendy, Hook—"

"So that's where Hook went," Tink said as she perused Peter's kitchen and living area. Something was missing. Or rather, someone. She turned back to Peter. "Where's Wendy? I thought she'd be here."

Peter smirked. "With me?"

Tink huffed and rolled her eyes. "Yes, with you. That lousy girl was always at your side, taking up unnecessary space." Space Peter should've shared with Tink.

Peter chuckled. "She married Hook."

Tink's head whipped around to face Peter. "*Hook*? Is she mad?"

"He reformed, as have I," Peter said, shrugging. "He's not so bad a fellow now. They have a little girl. He's actually a rather good father."

"Hmm," Tink said, resuming her meandering. So long as Wendy wasn't with Peter, Tink didn't care what had happened to her. "You said you've changed?"

He exhaled and rubbed the back of his neck. "Yes. I was immature and thought only of myself."

Tink raised an eyebrow. "But not now?"

Peter shook his head. "How did you find me?"

"It took some time, but I found you. There's a sort of . . ." How could she describe it? "Aura you give off. I followed its energy."

Peter squinted. "There's no magic here."

"Energy doesn't need magic to exist, you stupid boy."

He smirked. "And you found me so you could spook me at my cabin and break into my condo."

Tink gasped. "How did you know that was me at the cabin?"

"I'm using deductive reasoning. Also, you just confirmed my suspicion."

She pouted. He'd figured her out again. Like always. "Yes, you've always been clever."

"I should make you clean up the mess you made."

Tink turned to him. "What mess? I was only on the roof."

Peter's eyebrows scrunched. "The wood pile and the ice melt—that wasn't you?"

She flipped her hand. "No. Why would I want to make a mess? That's ridiculous." She sauntered to his couch and let herself fall onto the soft cushions. "Some snow fell when I moved to see you better, but that's all."

Peter followed her. "Why don't you make yourself at home?" he deadpanned.

"I shall do as I please." She propped her dainty feet on his ottoman but was suddenly hoisted from her spot by Peter's firm arms.

She swung her limbs around, hitting and kicking him wherever she could. "Put me *down*!" she shouted.

Peter chuckled. "Still hot tempered." He glanced around his arms at the rest of her form, causing her neck to heat up. "Still the same everything, except your height." He smirked.

Oh, that stupid yet ever so attractive smirk of his. Tink humphed while fisting her hands at her sides. "You idiot," she seethed. "Put me down."

He did so and she promptly fell onto the couch in a rather undignified manner to the sound of Peter laughing.

Fine. Time to enact her plan. She stood, dusted herself off, and sauntered toward his front door. She heard his footsteps behind her. Good—let him follow her for once.

"Where're you going?" he asked, still chuckling when he caught up to her. "You just got here."

She turned and tilted her head up to meet his magnetizing eyes. He truly had grown tall.

"It's like our game of hide and seek, Peter. Which you were always terrible at." She folded her arms.

He chuckled. "I wasn't *that* bad at it."

"Pft." Tink rolled her eyes. "You found me maybe three times out of ten. You usually got bored and stopped looking for me."

"Well," Peter spread his arms out. "You found me."

He thought the game was over, did he?

"Indeed," she said, stepping toward him and running her hand down his solid chest, her fingers burning with the feel of it. "You've always loved games. Now it's my turn to hide." She then bunched his shirt as though to pull him closer, his eyes widening as her lips grew nearer to his.

"Let's see how far you get this time," she whispered. She then shoved him, causing him to stumble and fall onto his back. Then she placed a foot on his chest, sensing his heart pounding through her shoe. "Will you give up again? Or will you see it through like the reformed man you claim to be?"

She lifted her foot off his chest and stepped to the door. "You have two days." She glared at his prostrate form. "I dare you to come find me."

She exited his condo and slammed the door behind her. "See how it feels to be the one to seek," she muttered as she trotted down the condo porch steps.

Her heart teetered between victory and anxiety.

Would he come for her or would he abandon her again?

~

What was that? And why was Peter's heartbeat rushing like a waterfall? He thought of Tink pinned beneath him, of her hand pulling on his shirt, and her foot on his chest while he lay on the ground.

She'd come after him. How long had it taken her to find him? He put himself in her situation and ran through her possible emotions when she realized he'd left: hurt, anger, jealousy, sadness. He hadn't meant to conjure any of those feelings in her, as he figured she'd become distracted enough to forget, as fairies usually did. He was immature back then— selfish and impulsive. He'd changed though.

He stared at the door Tink had slammed during her dramatic exit mere minutes ago.

Hide and seek. Oh, the fun they'd had in Neverland with that game. So many places to hide, such a thrill. Until he got bored searching for her. She'd been so small and so hard to find.

But Tink was a full person now as her prolonged stay in Reality had led to a loss of magic that had shifted her size. In Neverland, he'd often imagined what she would look like if she were his size. She'd stayed petite. Same fiery eyes, light hair, and full, pouty lips that spat feisty words at him.

His heart pinched thinking of the struggle she must've faced while searching for him. She'd said she found him through his aura, his energy. Was that the hair-raising influence *her* energy gave *him*?

He would take her dare and find her. His sense of duty wouldn't let her be alone again. And when he found her, he'd be curious to see if she felt the same pull toward him as he did to her.

Two days. He could find her in two days.

He slept fitfully that night, dreaming of a cougar charging full speed at him as he stood frozen in a snowdrift. Just before the cougar plowed into him, he awoke in a cold sweat. He sat up in bed before checking the time. Not yet eight in the morning.

He got up and got dressed in under five minutes, before grabbing an energy drink on his way out. When he got in his truck, he realized he had no idea where to start searching for Tink.

He shut his eyes and took a gentle inhale. Where had she hidden in Neverland? Sometimes she hid in full green trees, but the trees here were leafless in winter and would make a terrible hiding place. She had no wings to carry her up anymore anyway. And why would she be in a tree?

Other times she hid in Mermaid Lagoon, where she often taunted the mermaids out of jealousy. But there were no warm waterfronts or mermaids nearby.

Most often she hid among individuals—under a Lost Boy's hat or in the swarm of her Fae civilization.

Crowds. Perhaps she was among the hordes of people at a nearby ski resort. Only one way to find out. It'd been a couple weeks since he'd gone anyway.

He could stay focused on finding Tink while skiing.

~~~

But he couldn't stay focused. The slopes were among his favorite winter sports, and it was early afternoon before he realized he'd gotten distracted.

No, he could do this. He was a grown man and could focus on finding his . . . friend? How could he define their relationship? Tink used to be his sidekick, but Wendy made it perfectly clear that being in that position was no way to win a woman's heart. He wouldn't make that mistake twice.

Whatever their status was, he could find Tink and show her she wasn't insignificant, and that he wasn't the immature boy he'd been before. He could master this dare of hers.

He spent the rest of the day scanning the ski lodges at several resorts. In the evening, he walked Main Street, weaving in and out of restaurants, shops, and museums.

That sensation on the back of his neck hit twice, like what he'd experienced at his cabin, but he didn't see Tink anywhere. Fatigue hit around midnight, long after Main Street became empty.

As he slid into bed around one in the morning, he pondered over other possible places she could be. But sleep claimed him before any solution materialized.

⌘

Tink wondered if she ought to have made it easier for Peter to find her yesterday. She'd been among the mass of people wandering Main Street last night. She could tell the instant he'd sensed her energy—his head had jerked upright, and his eyes had darted everywhere.

She scowled. That's just what she'd done while looking for him. She'd searched high and low in this world, knowing his energy was nearby, but not knowing exactly where he was.

Her eyes narrowed. No, she wouldn't make it easy. She wanted him to understand what she'd gone through.

She could tell he was savvy to her possible location. He'd looked among highly populated places yesterday, probably remembering that she had hid among populated areas in Neverland. Maybe she should make the search harder, let him get a taste of the difficulty.

Her mind wandered to the moment she had found out he and the others had left her behind while they went to Reality. Her sight had blurred with jealousy, certain he'd left her behind so he could claim Wendy as his without her interference.

Her Fae clan had spent forever distracting her so she wouldn't go after him. She'd tried to forget him as long as she could until his absence pulled at her like a tether. She needed him—she *wanted* him.

Oh, that she hadn't attached herself to him for so long. She could still be with her clan, able to live as a fairy ought to.

But no. She'd gone and given her heart to him forever ago. And now he'd grown into a man whose allure outweighed even the most sought-after Fae man.

She imagined what it would've been like if Peter had kissed her as he had her pinned down, or when she'd fisted his shirt.

She'd imagined his kisses countless times. Such fantasies could never come to fruition with her as a tiny fairy. But now that she was his size—well, closer to his size since he stood at least head and shoulders above her. But still. She imagined those strong arms around her, holding her tight. His head tilted down to her . . .

But first he had to find her. Then he had to feel what she felt for him in return. He also needed to sincerely apologize for leaving her, but she'd take his kisses first and the apology second.

She straightened her green beanie and buttoned her matching peacoat. A love song played through her earbuds as she entered the mill of activity, shoppers coming and going through a local outlet mall.

Peter had been on the right track last night searching for her in the crowds. She hoped he would find her today—his last day.

At the same time, she wanted him to feel some of the suffering his deception had caused her.

She honestly didn't know what she'd do if he didn't find her. Should she have given him more time? She took him for a clever man who could accomplish such a thing within her given timeframe.

Would she simply leave if he didn't find her, or if he gave up? Except she truly wanted him to find her.

Oh, stupid emotions. Why must they be so complicated?

Peter searched additional ski resorts and other places he could think of that gathered large crowds but there was a palpable lack of that hair-raising sensation she gave him.

He face-palmed as he passed the outlet mall off the highway. Of course. If the sensation on his neck were any indication, Tink was somewhere in there. The apprehension followed as well. Were both sensations connected to Tink? Or was the apprehension tied to something different?

He drove to the outlet mall and parked his truck before hopping out, turning in a circle as though the right place to start would materialize.

His aimless steps took him to the middle of the parking area, and he jumped as a car honked at him.

The driver seemed familiar, but Peter's opportunity to study the man's face fled as the car sped away.

He decided he'd start at one end of the outdoor mall and work his way around the shops.

Shoe stores, candle stores, hat stores, stores selling bags, housewares, clothing, and almost every other type of merchandise passed Peter's eyes in a blur as he searched for Tink.

His stomach growled hours later, reminding him that he hadn't eaten all day. He spotted a food truck in a corner of the shopping area and strode toward it.

The apprehensive sensation hit him like a punch in the gut, feeling distinctly different from Tink's hair-raising sensation. Was he being followed by someone? He slowed his pace and tucked his hands into his wool coat pockets, risking a glance over his shoulder. Too many people to narrow down. He changed direction toward an art store where three people stood inside.

A minute after he entered the store, the familiar man from the parking lot came in. The apprehensive feeling burned in his chest. This game of hide and seek had gained an unwelcome player.

~~

What is Peter doing in an art store? Tink wondered. She stood in the doorway of a shop two doors down to satisfy her curiosity.

Peter darted out of the art store and Tink pulled her hat lower. It was unnecessary since Peter went in the other direction. When he was perhaps four stores away, she slipped into the crowd to follow him from a distance. His long strides made the task tricky, and she trotted at times to keep him in her line of sight. He entered a crowded department store and Tink sighed with relief—he was back to looking for her in crowds.

The sight of his determined countenance loosened her resolve for revenge. At that moment, all she desired was reconciliation. And his kisses. Perhaps she should enter the store as well and make it simple for him to spot her. Then they could move forward, whatever that looked like.

Yes, surely he'd learned his lesson by now after traveling all over the area searching for her.

She straightened her shoulders, her legs taking her toward the department store. Shoppers passed her from the other direction, some bumping into her amid the mass of people. She thought nothing of it until a man's hand tugged her arm, causing her to follow him the other way.

"There you are," the stranger said with an American accent. "Let's head this way."

"You're mistaken, sir," she said, rotating her arm to free herself, but the hand squeezed harder. She turned her face to the man, who pulled her along through the crowded sidewalk.

"Let go," she snapped. Who did he think he was to force her like this?

The man turned to face her, and alarm hit her senses. He smirked at her with an ill-intending expression.

They neared a break between buildings, and he tugged her around the back of the stores, where he tossed her to the gravel-strewn ground next to a dumpster.

Fear turned to anger at being shoved to the filthy ground. "How dare you treat me like this." She moved to stand but stopped when the man slipped a gun out of his pocket and aimed it at her face.

He chuckled and narrowed his eyes. "Hang tight for a minute, honey. I'm gonna need you for a bit." He handed her a pair of handcuffs. "Put these on or you'll have a hole in your head."

Tink swallowed through a dry throat and did as she was told.

Peter scanned every person in the busy clothing store, but no Tink. He was close—he could feel it.

He exited the store just as a call came through his cell phone. He answered it, and the apprehension immediately seized his chest again. "This is Peter."

"Hey, Peter," a man's chipper voice said. "I've got a friend of yours here."

Peter heard a female voice call for him in the background. Tink?

"How can I help you, sir?" Peter asked.

"Well, I've got a score to settle with you, and I've also got the leverage to convince you to follow my instructions."

How could the man sound so calm? Was he insane?

"He's got a gu—" Tink's voice carried before the sound of a car door slamming cut her off.

A text message pinged on Peter's phone with a rural address.

The man's voice became sinister. "Meet me at the address if you want your girlfriend back alive."

The call ended. Peter's heart pulsed in his throat. He ran to his truck as fast as he could, then sped out of the shopping area while making a phone call.

The address led Peter to a deserted, snow-covered cabin outside the city limits, the wood and shingles having been claimed by insects and vines long ago.

He nudged the front door open with his foot, and the exaggerated creaking it made would've been comical if not for the sight of Tink sitting on the floor inside, cuffed and gagged.

His heart sighed with relief—she was alive.

She straightened while trying to say something he couldn't understand through her gag. Her head shook fiercer, her eyes growing wider the closer he approached her.

The door slammed shut behind him. Peter whipped around to find the man from the parking lot standing in front of the door, a gun pointed at Peter's chest.

Peter used steady breathing to keep his mind clear.

"Recognize me?" the man asked, stone-faced.

Peter narrowed his eyes, his mind searching through the many people he knew.

Recognition hit. "You left the group on the last trek."

The man scowled. "*You* left *me* behind."

Peter's heart pinched. First Tink had been left behind, now this man—Darrell.

But Darrell's missing status had been his own fault, not Peter's.

Peter's face hardened. "What do you want?"

The man's scowl fled and he laughed. "Revenge, of course. You left me to die." He gestured the gun toward Tink, setting Peter's heart skittering. "I'll take something you care about to prove a point." He shrugged. "Then I'll shoot you."

216

Peter lifted his chin. "How do you know this woman is important to me?"

The man chuckled. "She's been following you for days. To me, that says there's something between you two."

Peter turned his eyes to Tink to convey his determination to keep her safe, and she released her breath. But she was shivering.

Peter needed time. He returned his attention to Darrell. "Why did you leave the group?"

"I'm a photographer," Darrell said as though that should be enough. "I needed photos for a contest and social media posts, and this rugged area's full of award-winning and follower-hungry potential. It's why I signed up for your tour in the first place—I knew I'd get tons of material. But when you led us on beaten paths away from the ideal locations, I had to venture off by myself."

Peter fought the urge to roll his eyes. "You asked to head into other areas, and I explained why we had to stay on the path. Those ecosystems thrive better when we stay out of them, and we stay safe following the trail."

Darrell shook his head. "You didn't listen to me. Then you took the group and left me."

Anger heated Peter's chest. "You *chose* to go another direction, and when you chose to do that, you chose the consequences that followed."

"You left me out there to freeze to death!" Darrell shouted. The gun shook in his unsteady hand.

Peter wondered how much longer he could hold this lunatic off while keeping himself and Tink alive. He placed his hands out placatingly in front of him. "You were out there in the cold for hours—it

217

must've been frightening on your own. It's fortunate the rescue team found you when they did."

Darrell grunted while he motioned the gun from Peter to Tink. "Go sit next to her. That way it'll be easier to shoot you both."

Before Peter could check himself, he scoffed. "You want me to make this easy for you?"

"You didn't make my survival in the snow easy," Darrell yelled. "Now go."

Peter took tentative steps backward, keeping his eyes on Darrell as he knelt next to Tink.

～

Tink pondered her current situation. This man demanded revenge from Peter, assuming he'd been intentionally left behind. Tink had felt justified to exact revenge on Peter for leaving *her* behind.

Revenge. What an unnecessary choice. Her certainty of being in the right had dissolved during the last hour. She and Peter had a gun in their faces because a man justified himself in taking revenge. Though it seemed he was in the wrong to begin with.

Tink glanced at Peter, sending him an apology with her eyes. If these were their last moments, she needed to express her contrition, even without words.

Oh, how ridiculous she'd been! Putting him up to this life-size game of hide and seek, just so she could prove a point. She'd found him, shouldn't that have been enough? Now she'd lose any chance of a future with him, along with her life.

Peter seemed to understand her expression. But rather than responding with worry or fear, he shifted to kneel in front of her, facing Darrell, blocking the gun's access to her.

Then he turned and winked. What on earth was there to wink about at a time like this?

Before her mind could come up with any further ideas, Darrell called for their attention.

He aimed the gun at Peter's face. Tears spilled over Tink's eyes as the blood started to drain from her head.

Darrell smirked. "Fine, you can go first. Here's to revenge, Peter."

Tink shut her eyes, and it seemed to take forever for the gun to go off. But instead of a gun, the door banged open, knocking Darrell over and sending his gun flying across the rotting wood floor.

"Freeze! Police!" Five police officers filled the room, guns drawn toward a cowering Darrell who crouched with his hands covering his head.

Peter released a sigh. "About time they showed up."

The police handcuffed Darrell as he shouted threats and offensive words at them, then they pulled him out of the cabin to a police car.

Peter shifted around to face Tink, untying the cloth around her mouth, pulling out his pocket knife, and picking the lock on her handcuffs.

Once free, Tink fell into his arms, which encircled her in a cocoon of refuge. His warmth dissolved her anxiety, bringing coherent thought forward.

She turned her head to look up at him, still in his arms. "How did you know the police were coming?"

He gave her a cocky grin that set her heart wild while brushing her messy hair out of her face, sending icy fire through her body. "I called the police on my way to you."

Tink huffed a relieved laugh. "Always clever."

"I wasn't about to face this lunatic alone." He searched her eyes while holding her face in his hands, then moved his head closer to hers. "And I wasn't about to leave you behind again."

His lips hovered over hers and Tink felt her body shudder.

Peter pulled away. "You're hurt," he said, standing.

Tink's eyes stuttered open. "What? No." She wanted him and those lips of his back where they belonged, right over hers.

"Let's get you to my condo."

Tink protested until Peter pulled her into his arms, one arm behind her back, the other under her knees. Her heart sputtered as she took in his masculine, woodsy scent. She exhaled. "Lead the way."

She imagined the lovely things they could do at his home, cuddling on his couch being her favorite idea. Then he'd move in for another kiss, and she'd—

"Ow!" she said as Peter abruptly deposited her in his truck.

"Stay here for a moment while I finish with the police," Peter instructed before returning to the cabin.

He was the master of the unexpected. Tink smiled. That was one of the things she absolutely adored about him.

⌇

After Darrell was hauled away by the police and the necessary procedures had settled, they were given permission to leave, much to Tink's relief.

It was several silent minutes into the car ride when Tink couldn't keep her apology in anymore.

She closed her eyes and shook her head. "I'm so sorry, Peter."

She heard him chuckle and opened her eyes to find him casting an amused glance her way. "What horrible crime have you committed now, Tink?"

She hit his shoulder. "How can you be silly after all this? I was so angry when you left—"

Peter nodded. "Hence the hide and seek tournament."

"Shut up, let me finish." Tink crossed her arms. "I wanted you to feel sorry by putting you through my impossible game."

Peter scoffed. "I nearly found you on my own—it wasn't impossible."

She turned to him and scowled. "You found me handcuffed with a rag around my mouth in a forsaken cabin while a madman pointed a gun at me."

"I had a little help with the address."

Tink's heart softened remembering the moment Peter entered that horrid cabin. "I'm grateful you found me. Especially in those circumstances."

Peter chuckled, setting Tink's nerves going, but piquing her curiosity. "What?"

"Surely that isn't the most dangerous situation you've ever been in?"

"Well, there was Hook, and the crocodile ..."

Peter nodded. "And the mermaids."

"Splashing water on me hardly counts as danger."

Peter tilted his head side to side. "Still. You've been through worse."

"And you were always there to help me."

Peter was silent for several moments as they traveled the winding road back to the city. "I'm sorry I left you behind, Tink."

She shifted her eyes to her lap. "I'm sorry I set out to exact revenge on you. I'm just as bad as Darrell."

"No, no. You're *much* worse than Darrell," Peter joked.

Tink hid a smile while her eyes followed the sights out her window.

Peter cleared his throat. "Shall we start over?" he asked as they pulled up to his condo.

The car stilled as he turned off the ignition and Tink shook her head. "There's too much I want to remain in place for us to start over." She pursed her lips while pondering. "How about a continuation?"

"A new adventure?"

"Yes, that sounds better than starting over." Tink pulled her knees in to face him better from her seat. "What do you have in mind?"

Her heart began to pound at his deviously attractive smile. "Have you ever been to Las Vegas?"

~

"Are we there yet?" Tink whined from the passenger seat. Peter wondered how she could be so tempting when she was irritated.

"It's just over this hill here," he answered as he drove down the interstate, anxiously hoping Tink was willing to take on this adventure he had in mind.

Tink exhaled. "It's so dark and it's only six-thirty. It feels so late already."

"That's because it's February. It gets darker earlier."

"What will we do when we—oh!"

They crested a rise in the road, and the glitter and sparkle of Las Vegas shone ahead of them.

Peter would never tire of this sight. "Impressive, isn't it?"

"Nearly as sparkly as the Fae Quarter." Tink turned her head to face him. "Was this the adventure you had in mind?"

"Part of it." He cleared his throat to dislodge the words that were stuck there and decided to keep them in until they reached the city limits.

That came too quickly as they exited the freeway, and panic sent his words tumbling out incoherently. "So adventures and futures, right? They can go together. Like us. And Valentine's Day. Or rather, Valentine's night, since it's dark outside. And ..."

Tink angled her body toward him. "What's got your tongue tied, Peter?" She smirked and his heart pounded against his ribcage.

Had he been capable of love in Neverland? He remembered only loving himself at the expense of everyone else's well-being. When Tink broke into his condo he'd been shocked but not upset. A different sensation had coursed through his body that night. Attraction, certainly. And then she'd sent him on her hide and seek game, and he couldn't pass up the chance to prove himself to her. Then she'd been in danger, and he would rather have lost his own life than allow harm to come to her.

Attraction, trust, sacrifice. Love.

Did she love him back? One way to know.

223

He rubbed the back of his neck with a sweaty palm. "I love you."

He chanced a glance at Tink, whose wide eyes and pursed lips conveyed her surprise. Her shallow breaths set her chest rising and falling rapidly.

Peter ran a hand through his hair after moments of silence. "Say something, Tink."

"Pull over."

"What do you—"

"Pull over, you nitwit." She pointed to a restaurant at the side of the road.

Peter obeyed, navigating the truck to an obscure parking spot then turned to Tink. "I didn't mean to upset—"

His apology was cut off by Tink's lips on his, her hands running over his torso and neck. He figured the apology was unnecessary and followed her lead.

Minutes passed where words were unnecessary. Tink lifted her head before running her fingers over his mouth. "I've waited an eternity for you to say that to me."

Peter huffed a surprised laugh as his arms tightened around her waist. Dare he venture forth with this adventure? He wanted to. More than anything.

"Marry me, Tink."

Her eyes darted between his, smile creases lining the corners of her eyes as a tear fell down her soft cheek. "Is this the adventure you had in mind?"

"Mm-hm," he said before placing a soft kiss on her mouth.

"I love you," she murmured through their kiss.

She loved him back?

Peter pulled away. "Woo!" It came before he could stop himself. To love and to be loved in return—what an exhilarating adventure.

Tink chuckled as she rested her hand against his chest. "How soon can we be married?"

Peter tilted his head down, his eyes on hers. "Is that a yes?"

Tink rolled her eyes. "Of course it is, you silly man."

Peter groaned and pulled her to him, his kiss hungry for a lifetime with the feisty words her lips would say.

He glanced at the dashboard clock. "An hour," he breathed.

Tink lifted her head, then tilted it in question, raising an eyebrow.

Peter caught his breath. "We have an hour before our wedding appointment."

"You set an appointment *before* asking me to marry you?" Tink asked, sounding more surprised than angry.

Peter shrugged. "I couldn't resist. I figured if you said no, I'd just cancel the appointment and wallow in misery forever."

Tink sat up. "Well, what are you waiting for? Let's go."

Peter shifted in his seat to take control of the car, but Tink was back in his arms without warning.

"Maybe we could stay just another minute more," she reasoned.

Peter was happy to comply.

⚬⚬⚬

Their marriage ceremony seemed to take forever to Tink, though it was only twenty minutes from the time they entered the building till the officiator pronounced them husband and wife.

Peter pulled Tink into their hotel room and she shoved the door closed while pulling him flush against her.

"I'm sorry it took me so long to understand my love for you," he whispered.

She smiled against his lips. "This was worth waiting for."

The End

ACKNOWLEDGEMENTS

I hope you enjoyed the stories of our Neverland friends and their adventures in our world. If you liked it, feel free to leave a review. (Actually, please leave a review if you liked it, because authors love to hear that you really liked their books. Hopefully it's a nice review.)

Thanks to everyone who listened to me talk about this second edition (which is a lot of people).

Thanks to my editor, KaTrina Jackson of Eschler Editing. Your feedback drove this story forward and pushed me to rethink how things could go for these characters. This version wouldn't be what it is without your help.

Thanks to all the folks at Eschler for your guidance and patience as I started from Square One on this revision. You guys are awesome.

Thank you to my hermanas for telling Peter Pan about my book when we saw him at Disney. The look on his face when I told him he grew up in the story? Priceless.

My husband must needs be thanked for many things. I talked his ear off about the story and he willingly(?) listened. His support bolstered me through several times of doubt. He also did some final edits of the book and helped me bend a few plot ideas to improve the story.

Finally, and certainly most importantly, thanks to God for carrying me through this. I admittedly prayed throughout these revisions and edits, and I felt His help in this journey. He is the giver of all good things.

ABOUT THE AUTHOR

When she's not writing (which admittedly comes in random waves), Mindy is often found reading, eating chocolate, being with her family, reading some more, and listening to Owl City. She lives in the Intermountain West with her husband, four kids, three cats, two reptiles, and a cockatiel.

You can follow her shenanigans in several areas...

Instagram: @mindylemieux

Visit her website to join her newsletter: mindylemieux.com

Email her at authormindy10@gmail.com

ALSO BY MINDY

"Meet Me at the Cemetery"
a spooky, clean romance short story

"I'm Not a Supervillain"
a superhero clean romance short story

Coming in 2026: "Madness in Wonderland"
a steampunk Wonderland clean romance novel